Sophia

PRAISE FOR *Sophia*

"This book will reawaken you to the sheer pleasure of reading. It has everything I look for—great characters, a plot that keeps you guessing, and lots of romance."

—REBECCA JAMISON, author of *Sense and Sensibility: A Latter-day Tale, Emma: A Latter-day Tale*, and *Persuasion: A Latter-day Tale*

"Kremser whisks the reader into scene after vivid scene as this delightful romance unfolds in the English countryside. Sometimes she frightens us, often perplexes us, but always provides us with a great deal of entertainment. Sophia and Alex's love story is a must-read."

—ANNETTE HAWS, award-winning author of *Waiting for the Light to Change* and *The Accidental Marriage*

Sophia

PAULA KREMSER

SWEETWATER
BOOKS

AN IMPRINT OF CEDAR FORT, INC.
SPRINGVILLE, UTAH

ISBN 13: 978-1-4621-1482-5

Published by Sweetwater Books, an imprint of Cedar Fort, Inc.
2373 W. 700 S., Springville, UT 84663
Distributed by Cedar Fort, Inc. www.cedarfort.com

LIBRARY OF CONGRESS CATALOGING-IN-PUBLICATION DATA

Kremser, Paula, 1978- author.
 Sophia / Paula Kremser.
     pages cm
  Summary: Sophia Spencer is excited about an unexpected opportunity to spend the season in London. However, growing up in a small village has not prepared her for the hidden rules and constant engagements of London society, and when she takes a break from a ball and rests in a handy bedroom she finds herself in a compromising situation.
  ISBN 978-1-4621-1482-5 (perfect : alk. paper)
  1. London (England), setting. I. Title.
  PS3611.R467S66 2014
  813'.6--dc23
                        2014013412

Cover design by Kristen Reeves
Cover design © 2014 by Lyle Mortimer
Edited and typeset by Melissa J. Caldwell

Printed in the United States of America

10 9 8 7 6 5 4 3 2 1

This book is dedicated to my sister, Josie,
for helping me every step of the way.

Prologue

Lady Atkinson had lied to her daughter Nora. It was a small lie, really. As Lady Atkinson had pulled on her gloves, Nora came into the room and asked where she was going. She answered that she was visiting Mrs. Morris this morning, a friend whose declining health had confined her to bed. But Lady Atkinson had no intention of visiting Mrs. Morris.

She had to lie. There really was no other alternative. If she told Nora the truth—where she was really going today—Nora would have been furious. Lady Atkinson was actually on her way to an appointment with her solicitor in order to cut her daughter out of her will.

She had been contemplating this for some time and finally realized that she had to act, or all her hard-earned money would be lost. Lady Atkinson had been experiencing terrible stomachaches recently and the remedies her doctor had provided had done nothing. She didn't know how much longer she had, but the real push had come last month when Nora's husband, Lord Bloomfield, had departed at night for the country to escape his creditors. Lady Atkinson had not spent half her life carefully managing her wealth just to let it fall into the hands of her unworthy son-in-law. Just thinking about it made her ill . . . more ill than she was already. Subterfuge seemed to make her condition worse; the bumping of the carriage wasn't helping either. She pressed her hands to her middle, trying to lessen the pressure and pain. Once today's errand was behind her, she expected to feel at least a little better.

Nora had been living with Lady Atkinson for the last month rather than departing to the country with her husband, so it wasn't easy for Lady Atkinson to come and go without her daughter's knowledge. Luckily, when she had lied this morning, Nora hadn't seemed suspicious. Oh, but she would be livid when she found out. But if everything went according to plan, Lady Atkinson would be in her grave before that happened.

She climbed out of the carriage and entered the solicitor's office with purpose. Today she would save her carefully amassed fortune by keeping it out of the hands of her daughter and son-in-law, and Mr. Wilson was just the man to help her complete the task.

She emerged from Mr. Wilson's office nearly two hours later, her stomach still aching, but she felt as if a huge weight had been lifted off her shoulders. Although he had resisted some of her unusual requests at first, Mr. Wilson helped her arrange everything to her satisfaction, and she felt that her money was as safe as it could be.

Lady Atkinson was relieved, but she couldn't feel content, and she spent the short ride home reflecting on how it had come to this. She was like so many parents: she wanted her children to be as happy as she was and thought that if they had the same experiences she had had, they would be just as happy.

She and her husband had married at the arrangement of their parents. They met for only the second time on their wedding day. But shortly thereafter, they had formed a strong attachment and enjoyed a happy marriage. She wanted the same thing for her daughters, and planning whom they would marry had been a favorite pastime of hers. Sometimes she favored this viscount or that earl, and she had always been on the lookout for an eligible duke.

When her eldest daughter, Nora, came of age, she and Lord Atkinson had arranged her marriage to Lord Bloomfield, who had just recently stepped into the title after his father's death. It was a happy day for Lady Atkinson when Nora became Lady Bloomfield. But that was the last time things had gone according to plan. Unfortunately, Nora did not have the same experience as her mother. She never fell in love with Lord Bloomfield and rather grew to despise him. Her mother watched with disappointment as Nora and her son-in-law became estranged.

At the center of their marital discord were their mounting financial troubles. Nora's husband was a poor manager who lived in excess of his means. They never had children, which made the problem worse. Once Lord Bloomfield felt certain that there would be no heir, he cared even less about maintaining what he had for future generations. After much inner turmoil on the subject, Lady Atkinson knew she couldn't possibly leave her carefully managed fortune to her daughter and son-in-law; it would amount to nothing in only a few short years if left to them.

Her other two daughters had both gone against her wishes by marrying men who should have been far beneath their notice. She had not recognized either of them after their marriages. Her daughter Amelia had left for America with her husband, which was almost worse than marrying beneath her. She didn't know if she had any grandchildren from Amelia. But of her daughter Sarah, she was more informed. She knew that Sarah—who had married a man who *could* have been a gentleman but *chose* to be a country doctor—had died along with her second baby in childbirth, leaving only a two-year-old daughter behind.

That girl, Sophia, was eighteen now and had apparently been raised to be a fine young lady. Lady Atkinson had found out through discreet enquiries to a former governess of young Sophia that she was being given an education befitting any young lady who belonged to the high society of the *ton* in London. Lady Atkinson would never forgive Sophia's father, Mr. Spencer, for having the audacity to marry Sarah and turn her into a country doctor's wife, but at least he had fulfilled his duty to his only child.

Lady Atkinson wished she had another option, but she had no other descendants whom she would trust with her money, so she had chosen her only granddaughter, Sophia Spencer, as her heir. She had doubts, of course, and she worried that her money might still be wasted, but she had done everything in her power to prevent that. The rest was up to fate.

One

Sophia Spencer bent her head over her sewing project and then leaned back again so she wouldn't block the light from the lamp to her right. She disliked sewing by lamplight, but this was the last of the dresses she had volunteered to make, and if she could finish this evening, then she could go riding tomorrow with a clear conscience. The other ladies in the neighborhood had also been sewing in their spare time over the last month so that when Reverend Henley went to Sheffield the following Monday, he could deliver the entire batch to the foundling home.

When Reverend Henley had asked the ladies in the parish to offer their services, Sophia had, of course, volunteered. She had signed up to sew six dresses—twice as many as Martha Bullock, who had signed up before her—and signed her name with a flourish. The pattern wasn't complicated, but the stitches seemed to never end. She regretted signing up for so many, but she wouldn't shirk her duty. Besides, helping orphans sounded like a good thing to do. When she had stepped into the shop yesterday and been cornered by Martha, it had sounded quite grand to announce that she couldn't possibly have prepared a song to perform at Mrs. Gibbs's because she was *so* busy making dresses for the dear orphans. Sophia always enjoyed putting Martha in her place; she just wished all this sewing hadn't taken up so much of her free time. Not the time practicing another boring song for another boring neighborhood party at Mrs. Gibbs's, but time that could have been spent outdoors riding her horse, Pearl. The weather had turned nice two days ago, and Sophia was determined to finish the sewing tonight. She had given her time much more charitably during the last few weeks of constant rain.

Despite the weather's turn for the better, evenings were still quite chilly, and she was glad of the warmth and the light from the fire as she and her father whiled away the evening hours. Her father was reading the latest news from town and commenting occasionally on some interesting thing or other, while Sophia continued her even row of stitches.

Mr. Spencer had lived in London for a short period of his life and had maintained his habit of reading the news every week. For Sophia, it didn't mean much. She had never even seen London.

Suddenly her father sat forward in his chair and said, "Oh my goodness." This was quite the declaration of surprise from her normally subdued father. Sophia looked up in interest, but he continued reading. She knew from experience that he wouldn't communicate until he had finished reading whatever interesting article he had come across. So Sophia waited patiently for him to look up. When he did, he had a wary look, as if he was worried what her reaction would be when he told her. Her curiosity was now truly piqued, and she demanded, "Out with it, Father. What's the bad news?"

Her father shifted in his seat but got right to the point. "Well,

Sophia, I'm just not at all sure how you will feel about it, but apparently your grandmother has recently passed."

Sophia leaned back in her chair and let her sewing fall to her lap. She pulled her lower lip between her teeth and thought about how she felt. She felt a tinge of sadness, but nothing at all like when Grandmother Spencer had passed away when she was ten. But she certainly wasn't relieved or happy either. Her sadness was just a regret inside her, that she hadn't ever tried to heal the rift with her mother's mother, and now there would never be an opportunity. She had somehow felt sure that she would accomplish that at some point.

She had imagined the scenario many times, with many variations. She would travel up to London and stay with a friend—a non-existent friend at this point, but that was a minor detail—then she would happen to meet her grandmother at a fine ball, where she would be admired and talked about by all. Everyone would wonder who the new mysterious beauty was. Her grandmother would speculate along with the rest of the crowd. Then when word reached her ears that the most elegant young woman in the room was her disowned granddaughter, she would faint dead away. And when Sophia herself produced smelling salts to revive her, Grandmother would have tears in her eyes as she begged forgiveness for her hard heart.

Tears came to Sophia's own eyes as she thought of the touching scene that would now never be.

Sophia's tears lasted only a few moments. She was sad for only what might have been, not for the passing of a woman she had never known. So she replaced the wetness in her eyes with a rueful smile. "I wish I could have known her, but she prevented it. Well, we've discussed the whole situation before; I suppose there's no need to say all the same things over again." And with that, Sophia turned back to her sewing.

Mr. Spencer had been closely watching his expressive daughter as he gave her the news of her grandmother's passing to see how she would react. The last thing he had expected was to see tears in her eyes. He had rather been expecting a bit of anger at the distant grandmother who had refused to know her only granddaughter. He had expected a quick retort of "good riddance!" rather than any sorrow.

William Spencer was reminded again that his precious daughter was really a grown woman now. Her mature reaction proved that. The evidence of it was all around him, though he tried to ignore it most of the time. Even now she was sewing away for some poor orphans, something that in the past he would have had to bribe her to do. He, too, sighed in sadness, not at the passing of his daughter's grandmother, but at the passing of time.

He watched for several moments as she continued on with her work, seemingly putting the whole thing out of her mind. This was a bit uncharacteristic of Sophia. He hated to admit that she had any faults, but if pressed he would have reluctantly said that Sophia was a bit self-absorbed. Really, the fault was probably his for spoiling her when she was young. As she entered her teenage years, it seemed to grow worse. Sophia always thought about herself first, but Mr. Spencer hadn't been overly worried. Youth were, typically, a selfish lot. Still, he had gently been trying to direct his daughter away from these selfish tendencies. He'd had varied success.

But now, when he had fully expected her to carry on and on about the injustice of her mother's family and how unfairly they had treated her, Sophia had instead quietly accepted the situation. After bidding Sophia good night and retiring to his room, he realized that he would soon have to think about Sophia's future. But with a bit of selfishness of his own, he decided to put off thinking about that for a while. There was no rush on his part to find her a husband. He would enjoy this time with his only child for a while longer before disturbing their peaceful existence.

Two

The next morning, Sophia had completely recovered from the news. In fact, it barely crossed her mind. There were regrets, of course, but she wouldn't think about her departed grandmother today if she could help it. She had stayed up a bit late last night finishing that last dress. Now came her reward. She was going to enjoy the late spring warmth that she had been longing for through the last several weeks of rain. She was going to ride her horse.

At breakfast, Sophia checked with her father that he wouldn't need Pearl today. Father's work as a doctor kept him in the village most days, but sometimes he would need to check on a patient who lived a few miles out. Then both horses would be hitched to their old carriage, and Sophia would spend a boring day on her own two feet.

Luckily, Pearl was all hers today, and Sophia carefully folded the six dresses she had sewn and wrapped them in a parcel to deliver to Reverend Henley's home before she ventured further from the village. She hurried out to the stable after her quick breakfast and found Pearl as ready to go as she was.

Sophia was forever embarrassed about her horse's name. When she was nine years old and her father had purchased the beautiful young horse, she had been given the job of naming it. She was a lovely pearly color of white, so Sophia had named her Pearl. For years she had regretted the ridiculous name, but she didn't want to admit it to anyone. Three summers ago she had privately called her Lightning for a while, thinking that was a much better name for a horse. One day, around that same time, she had been returning through Tissington commons from a lovely ride when her path had crossed Martha and a couple of other village girls. Staying put on the path directly in front of Sophia, Martha had remarked to her friends, "Well, if it isn't Miss Sophia Spencer and her legendary horse . . . *Pearl.*" The other girls had giggled at Martha's wit. But Sophia had shot her a bland smile. Her goal in life was to never let Martha goad her. Just because Martha was two years older than Sophia did not make her superior. The animosity between them was long-standing, and although Martha hit the mark by teasing Sophia about Pearl's name, Sophia knew she couldn't let Martha see that.

"I wouldn't have said 'legendary' myself, of course," Sophia had replied with mock humility. "But now that you've said it . . . well, I simply have to agree." And with that, she'd kicked her heels to Pearl's flanks, urging her up the steep bank and around the three girls, who let out startled screams. Sophia knew that a set-down followed by a quick departure was the best way to deal with Martha.

And so, despite the fact that Lightning was undoubtedly a better name for a legendary horse, Sophia didn't try to call her anything other than Pearl after that.

This morning, Sophia and Pearl set off at a quick pace, both ready to enjoy the day at full speed. It didn't last long though. The paths were quite muddy, and the ground was too soft from all the recent rain. Pearl had a hard time finding solid footing, so Sophia pulled her back to a slow trot for most of their ride. More than once, Sophia hopped off and walked her through a boggy marsh. After all her anticipation, it was a bit of a disappointing excursion. When she arrived home, she was tired and quite dirty.

The first thing she noticed upon her return was a carriage in front of her house. Sophia and her father often had visitors, but very few of them ever came in a carriage. Lord and Lady Fitzgerald had taken their children to the seaside, so it couldn't be them. Besides this wasn't their carriage. She was sure she had never seen those horses before, and the carriage was a plain yet expensive one. Strange. Who could it possibly be? She had to take care of Pearl, and then she would hurry in to satisfy her curiosity.

Thomas, their servant, met her at the stable door and reached for Pearl. "Hurry up, miss. You've a visitor. I'll take Pearl, and you best get inside quick. Yer father sent me out here to wait for you, and t' tell you not to keep yer visitor waitin'."

Thomas's urgency immediately transferred to Sophia and she rushed to the house, completely forgetting both her tiredness and the fact that she was covered in dirt.

Mr. Wilson, solicitor, was surprised to find himself enjoying a discussion of the newest measures taken by Lord Grenville to unite the government. He hadn't expected to find Mr. Spencer so well informed. His expectations had been altogether low. When Lady Atkinson had come to his office, she hadn't had any nice things to say about her son-in-law. For a moment he could almost forget that he was as far away from London as he had ever been and that he was anxious to get back. He had been born and bred in London, and though he frequently traveled to his various clients at their homes in the country, it wasn't to his taste. He always returned to London as quickly as he could.

The discussion was abruptly interrupted when the door to the sitting room burst open and a person who he assumed was a maid in the household rushed in. She came to an abrupt halt as she caught sight of Mr. Wilson. Her gaze moved questioningly to Mr. Spencer. Mr. Wilson also glanced toward his host.

Mr. Spencer seemed amused as he said, "Mr. Wilson, this is my daughter, Miss Sophia Spencer." Then turning to Sophia, he said, "Sophia, this is Mr. Wilson, he is your late grandmother's solicitor. He has some news for you concerning your grandmother's will."

Mr. Wilson's first thought upon being introduced to Miss Sophia Spencer was that Lady Atkinson had made a mistake in leaving all her worldly possessions to this unknown granddaughter. He had been expecting an elegant young lady to demurely enter the parlor. He hadn't recovered from his surprise or disappointment, but like any good solicitor, he hid this fact, cleared his throat, and said, "It's a pleasure to meet you, Miss Spencer."

For a moment she just looked back at him, apparently unsure what to say or do, and Mr. Wilson took the opportunity to assess her more fully. Her hair was a dark blonde, and most of it seemed to be uncontained. Her hazel eyes were wide, with a sparkle of curiosity in them. Her whole person seemed as though she belonged out of doors—pink cheeks, bright eyes, and a general impression of anticipation, like she was about to bounce or run. She wasn't at all like the delicate young ladies Mr. Wilson had seen all his life in London. And if he hadn't known she was eighteen, he would have guessed she was younger. She didn't look to be at all fit to manage a large fortune.

For a moment he considered just walking out without informing this uncultivated girl of Lady Atkinson's will. He knew his duty too well to truly consider such an option, but he was immensely relieved when she seemed to recollect her manners. "It is a pleasure to meet you too, Mr. Wilson. I'm sorry to have kept you waiting." She spoke elegantly, but it was her regal look as she curtsied a hello to Mr. Wilson that redeemed her in his mind; he could finally see a resemblance to Lady Atkinson.

She sat down directly across from Mr. Wilson, who wasted no time in delivering what was by then a memorized speech about how sorry he was for the loss of her dearly departed relation. He had delivered many such speeches, and usually there were tears of grief. This part always made him uncomfortable, but he found it best just to press on. He glanced at Miss Spencer, expecting to see a distraught look upon her face, but instead found that she didn't seem upset at all. Instead, curiosity and surprise were the most evident emotions.

Mr. Wilson hid his own surprise and continued, "Miss Spencer, Lady Atkinson showed her love for you to the last by naming you as her primary inheritor. She has bequeathed one thousand pounds to her daughter Lady Nora Bloomfield, who lives in London. One thousand pounds has been left to her other living daughter, Mrs. Amelia Brown, who has emigrated to America with her husband, but the will stipulates that she will only receive her inheritance if she returns to England. Your inheritance is everything remaining, which consists of investments for the most part, money in the funds, as well as your late grandmother's London townhouse and its contents."

Mr. Wilson paused here, expecting some sort of exclamation. When Miss Spencer just looked at him with wide eyes for several moments, he again continued to tell her what had befallen her in his succinct manner. "The house is yours to use immediately, but the investments will remain as they are until you marry or reach your twenty-fifth birthday, at which point you will gain control. You will receive a stipend each month of twenty pounds until you have met the terms of the trust."

Mr. Wilson's opinion of Miss Spencer increased in favor as he informed her of the rest of the terms of Lady Atkinson's will. Throughout the rest of his speech, she nodded her acknowledgement of his words and didn't interrupt him with questions. Despite his first impression of an uncultivated young lady, he could discern an intelligent look in her eye. Finally, he concluded by saying, "So of course, Miss Spencer, after the period of mourning has passed, I shall expect to meet with you to finalize the details."

Her surprise was once more evident to him, as if mourning her grandmother had never occurred to her. But she blinked several times and nodded again before replying, "Yes, Mr. Wilson. I will look forward to meeting with you after the mourning period. I hope you will stay and dine with us."

Mr. Wilson hesitated briefly, but the return trip ahead of him would only be dreaded more if he put it off. "No, thank you, Miss Spencer. It is a long journey back to London, and I wish to make a start immediately."

Sophia's father, Mr. William Spencer, was the grandson of a baronet and entitled to the life of a gentleman. His grandfather had had six sons and three daughters. William was the son of the baronet's third daughter. He was a practical man and had realized that for him to live the life of a gentleman, he would be quite dependent on others. So he chose a profession instead and had never regretted it. Sophia's mother, Sarah, had supported William in his decision, and as far as Sophia knew, she had never regretted it either.

Mr. Spencer was a well-respected doctor in Tissington and the surrounding villages. Most people Sophia knew looked up to her father as their superior. But when it came to the *ton* and a London Season, her father was on the very fringes. In his youth he had just stayed within fine society long enough to find Sarah Atkinson. They had quickly fallen in love and then Mr. Spencer had stolen Sarah away from the life she had led.

After Mr. Wilson's departure, Sophia and her father could talk of little besides her unexpected inheritance. As she was setting the table for their dinner, she suddenly stopped, plate in hand, and exclaimed to her father, "We should travel up to London together so I can have a Season! I never even dreamed such a thing would be possible for me, but now with grandmother's house and money, we could have a grand time there together." It was a perfect plan, and now that she thought of it, there was nothing else she wanted more.

Her hopes were quickly dashed. "I'm afraid I would be of little use to you, my dear," her father said. Sophia didn't understand why and gave him a questioning look, so he continued, "With my social situation, there wouldn't be many invitations forthcoming. Besides, I don't want to deprive the Tissington area of the best doctor in England."

This was said with a wink, and it brought a reluctant smile from Sophia. But for a while she was despondent because even with grandmother's inheritance, she couldn't traipse about London on her own.

Just over a fortnight later, all her problems were resolved when a letter from Lady Nora Bloomfield, her aunt, arrived.

The letter was so charming that Sophia was sure she had finally found a relation, besides her father, of course, whom she could love. Aunt Nora—as she wanted her dear Sophia to call her—offered to chaperone Sophia through her first London Season. It was exactly what Sophia was hoping for! This wasn't just helpful; it was an absolute necessity. The only thing that could have been better would be leaving for London right then. But Sophia would have to wait eight months because that was the time that her aunt specified for her to arrive—at the beginning of the Season.

Despite having to wait so long, Sophia bombarded her father with her enthusiasm. "Isn't it exciting news? And perfect timing too, for I was just beginning to despair of ever setting foot in London! Father, aren't you delighted for me?"

And, of course, her father said that, yes, he was delighted for her.

Later, as Sophia thought the matter over, she realized that the timing of her aunt's letter was too much of a coincidence. Father must have written to Aunt Nora and asked her to sponsor Sophia through the Season. What a difficult task that must have been. To contact her mother's family for the first time in more than fifteen years! The last time he had tried to contact them had been at her mother's death. No response had come. Sophia didn't know her father's feelings on this. He had told her of that first letter as a fact, very unemotionally, and only because she had been curious and had asked so many questions. But Sophia could just imagine how awful it must have been to be so insulted when he was still fresh in his grief.

And now, even all these years later, to write to Lady Bloomfield for a favor must have been a very unwelcome task for her father. Sophia had been joyful over something that must have caused her father pain. She resolved not to think so selfishly in the future. She had made similar resolutions before, but this time she was determined to succeed.

So she kept her enthusiasm in check around her father and told him how grateful she was for asking Aunt Nora for her help. He never did admit to doing so, but Sophia knew she was correct. She wrote an eager reply accepting her aunt's offer. All that was left to do was to be as patient as she could through the next eight months.

Three

Eight months and a fortnight later, Sophia Spencer arrived with her aunt, Lady Nora Bloomfield, at a ball hosted by Lord and Lady Everton. They were her aunt's dear friends apparently, which surprised Sophia when she saw they were much closer to her age than her aunt's. She had tried to seem alert as she spoke with them in the receiving line as she and Aunt Nora had arrived. She had no idea if she succeeded—she was just too tired.

Sophia had been in London for almost a fortnight, and she couldn't believe how exhausted she was. She never thought that attending parties would wear her out, but she felt much more in need of rest now than she ever had before. Sophia's life in the last two weeks felt, to her, like riding a horse galloping at full speed. Before arriving in London, she had been gently trotting along . . . no, a trot was a poor comparison. It was more like a walk, or possibly sitting on a horse that was standing perfectly still. To go from that sedate country life to this whirlwind of the London Season was overwhelming.

Standing next to her aunt in the Evertons' ball room, Sophia was just waiting for the night to end. The new gown she had on this evening was olive green, which wasn't a color she would choose to wear herself, but her aunt and her maid had insisted that it was the best of all her ball gowns. The gown was stiff, and the high lace collar scratched her neck, which was most noticeable when she danced and couldn't reach her hands up to push the lace aside.

Sophia had danced most of the dances and sat by some gentleman at supper, although she couldn't remember whom. It was unlikely that anyone she met tonight would even remember her. The most she had managed this evening was basic polite conversation.

As Sophia watched the dance in progress, it seemed that she could feel the room gently swaying. She tried to focus on one thing to stop the room from moving. It wasn't actually working, but she kept staring in the same direction.

She gazed, unseeing, across the room and thought about how she had come to be here and the last time she had felt comfortable and energetic. Probably it had been on the journey from Tissington, just before seeing London for the first time.

Her anticipation for the London Season had made it easy to bid farewell to her father and her home with a smile on her face. Sophia's father had intended to hire a maid to accompany her on the journey, but when speaking with Mrs. Smith, a matronly woman from a nearby village, he had found she intended a trip to London to visit her brother. So arrangements had been made for her and Sophia to travel together.

Sophia had loved the three-day journey to London. She and her father rarely traveled, and everything about the trip seemed like a novelty. But when the carriage rolled into London, she felt apprehensive for the first time. The number of people about was incredible to her. They dashed around, hardly noticing the passing carriage with Sophia and Mrs. Smith inside.

Mrs. Smith commented, "Not far now. We're on the outskirts of town."

Sophia was surprised. The outskirts of town were this busy and crowded? But Mrs. Smith had been right. They continued on and on with no break in the rows of houses on either side, and people, endless people, moved about.

It was loud and confusing, and Sophia kept her eyes open wide, trying to take it all in. With each passing mile, she became more nervous. How was she to cope with all this? It was so different from everything she had ever known. The people she saw all ignored one another; it was so different from her neighbors in Tissington. It was at that point that she felt a bit worried about how to act among these strangers.

Sophia took a deep breath and, with a shake of her head, tried to push these thoughts out of her mind. Mrs. Smith noticed the gesture and gave her an odd look, and Sophia admitted, "I feel a little daunted by all this."

Sophia waited for reassurance, but Mrs. Smith just turned to look out her window and replied, "Yes, London can be quite daunting." This caused another sinking feeling to come over Sophia.

Again, Sophia made a conscious effort to talk herself out of her worries. *It will be fine*, she thought. *I'll have Aunt Nora to help me, and I'm sure I'll quickly learn what's appropriate behavior in London.*

The carriage turned onto a very elegant street, and Sophia, taking it all in, again felt that she was in over her head. Her inheritance had surprised her initially, but the reality of it was even more surprising and overwhelming than she had first imagined. She told herself again that she would be fine and even whispered to herself, "Even if you're not, pretend you are."

Her stomach fluttered as the carriage slowed to a stop, and it took several deep breaths to calm herself. Sophia still didn't quite know how much she had inherited. Mr. Wilson's descriptions of her grandmother's investments had been confusing to say the least, and honestly, she hadn't paid much attention after he told her about her monthly stipend of twenty pounds every month. It was an enormous sum, and she had daydreamed about all the various ways it could be spent rather than listen to Mr. Wilson. In a response to a letter from his office, Sophia had informed him that she would be in London for the Season, and that she would take the earliest opportunity to call at his office. Hopefully a more thorough explanation would be given then. And she hoped to more thoroughly understand it.

As the driver helped her down from the carriage, she nearly slipped because she hadn't been able to look away from the beautiful home that belonged to her. She stood on the pavement and gawked at the mansion that was now her own home. How she wished her father could have been there. His presence would have put her at ease.

After another mental shake, Sophia quickly turned back to the carriage and said, "Thank you, Mrs. Smith, for accompanying me. It was lovely traveling with you." Simple as the statement had been, it was an exaggeration. It had been lovely traveling, but not because of Mrs. Smith.

Without getting out of the carriage for their farewell, Mrs. Smith simply replied, "And you, dear. Enjoy your Season."

Sophia was surprised at the feeling of being abandoned. But there wasn't any reason for Mrs. Smith to give her a fond farewell or even accompany her inside as Sophia wished she would.

Telling herself not to act like an ignorant country girl, Sophia ascended the stairs. She wanted so much to be loved by her Aunt Nora, and making a good first impression was especially important.

Sophia paused for a moment to make sure she felt ready to present herself in a poised and collected manner before ringing the bell. When a very fine butler answered, she introduced herself with the words she had practiced on her journey. "Hello, I am Miss Sophia Spencer. Is my aunt, Lady Bloomfield, in?"

The butler—who seemed much more intimidating than even Lord and Lady Fitzgerald's butler—looked at Sophia from head to toe before condescendingly opening the door wider for her to enter. "Please follow me, Miss Spencer." Without waiting to see if she complied, he led her to a sitting room and left without another word.

Sophia again felt weighed down by her new inheritance. Not by just the money and the house—she had also inherited this butler. Being a rich heiress must mean that an intimidating butler ran your house. She probably should have realized this before; then it wouldn't have come as such a surprise. What else was there that she should know but didn't? If she wanted to pass herself off as a fine young lady, she would have to learn quickly, and until then she would just have to pretend she knew what she was doing.

Several long minutes passed before a woman arrived. "Oh, my dear niece, Sophia! How happy I am to meet you at last!" the woman said as she entered the room. She came forward to clasp Sophia's hands.

Sophia was pleased to see that her aunt was the very description of elegance. Her hair was dark and stylishly pulled up, giving height to her appearance, with curls framing her face. She wore a deep red gown with ribbons adorning the waist and sleeves, and there was lace at the collar and sleeves that puffed out. Everything about Aunt Nora's appearance had volume to it, and Sophia felt small and flat in contrast. She had no memory of her mother and no pictures either. She wondered if her mother had survived, whether she would look like Aunt Nora.

"Aunt Nora, I'm so happy to meet you as well. It's so wonderful to finally know my mother's family."

"Oh, dear girl," Aunt Nora said sadly, "how difficult it must have been for you to be cut off through no fault of your own. How often I wished that we could meet, but your grandmother was so disappointed when Sarah married your father that she never allowed any contact. Even after your poor mother died." Aunt Nora put her arm around Sophia and led her to the sofa. "However, Mother seems to have forgiven Sarah at last by making you her inheritor." Aunt Nora smiled, but it seemed almost too sweet to Sophia.

"Well . . ." Sophia hesitated. "Yes, that's what I assumed as well, Aunt Nora. Grandmother must have forgiven my mother for her marriage in the end."

"Speaking of your mother, you don't look a thing like her. You must take after your father. Well, no matter. We'll soon have you looking lovely enough. I can hardly wait to take you to my dressmaker. We'll order new gowns for you in the latest fashion, and no one will be able to tell that you've come straight from the country."

Sophia had, in fact, spent a large sum of her monthly allowance on new clothing. And was wearing, for the first time, the nicest traveling dress she had ever owned. Until her aunt's comment, she felt quite sophisticated in her new attire. Trying to hide her surprise, she agreed with Aunt Nora. "Of course, Aunt. New gowns are just what I need."

After a short pause that felt uncomfortable to Sophia, her aunt asked, "How was your journey, Sophia? Isn't Tissington dreadfully far north?"

"Yes, the journey was quite long. Nearly three days." She had been hesitant to elaborate. It had been an exciting journey for her, but she didn't want to reveal the apprehension she had felt since arriving in London.

Their conversation continued in this stilted way, and Sophia looked forward to knowing her aunt well enough that their conversation could become easy and comfortable. Aunt Nora finally said, "You must be tired after such a long time in the carriage. I'll have Martin show you to your room. We'll have a light supper and then attend an evening party that my dear friend Mrs. Emery is hosting."

Sophia was startled at the thought of going out in company on her very first evening. She had expected to spend the evening getting acquainted with her aunt and uncle. She voiced her apprehension. "Aunt Nora, I haven't even met my uncle yet. Is Lord Bloomfield attending this evening's party as well?"

"Oh, no, certainly not. Even if he were in town, that's not the sort of thing that would interest him at all. Lord Bloomfield is at Smallbridge Hall." At Sophia's expectant look, her aunt continued, "It's our country estate in Suffolk. You won't meet him until the next time you come to London at least."

Sophia tried to appear as if this wasn't surprising news and nodded her head. "Oh . . . yes, maybe next time, then." Sophia wondered what other assumptions of hers would prove to be incorrect.

That first night was the beginning of a social life that Sophia had never imagined. Even just thinking about it all now as she stood next to her aunt in the Evertons' ballroom, she felt herself swaying with utter exhaustion.

Aunt Nora had a busy social schedule, and Sophia had been included in all of it. There were morning visits and afternoon teas. There were card parties and dinners. There were evening soirees and two balls already. Sophia heard some of the hostesses express their surprise at having her aunt accept their invitation. She assumed her aunt must get so many invitations every day that Aunt Nora must choose a few to accept of the many offered.

At first, this new London life had been quite fun and exciting. There were plenty of young ladies Sophia's age who were friendly and outgoing. They discovered right away that this was Sophia's first time in London, and then they had plenty of fun telling her all the best things to do in town. She had also been introduced to scores of young men. They were always so charming that she couldn't ever distinguish between them. She had talked and danced and played cards with many of them, but trying to remember later which face went with which name proved difficult.

Being constantly assailed with parties and various engagements every day was beginning to take its toll on Sophia. She might have been able to handle the busy whirlwind of activity if she had been getting more sleep. For the last few days especially, she had been extremely tired. Because there was no time during the day, her aunt scheduled her dress fittings for early in the morning. Aunt Nora had also seemed to think it necessary to buy from three different dressmakers. So for the last three mornings, the maid had come in quite early to rouse Sophia for her daily trip to another dressmaker for measurements. Her aunt had ordered more dresses in addition to the first set ordered on Sophia's second day in London. At first, Sophia was sure that her aunt was ordering too many, but after experiencing how frequently they went out, she wasn't sure it was enough. These morning fittings then seemed quite necessary to Sophia, and she had yawned through all three of them and tried to hide her yawns through three days of activities.

She didn't want to upset Aunt Nora in any way, but just before it was time to prepare for the ball, she couldn't help asking if she might skip it tonight. Before coming to London, she couldn't imagine not wanting to attend a ball. But nothing sounded better than a soft pillow under her heavy head at that moment. Aunt Nora, however, laughed and said, "Of course you can't miss the ball."

"Aunt, I am so tired," Sophia persisted. "Couldn't I just miss this one ball? I'm sure there will be others."

Sophia could tell that her aunt was not pleased when she waited for the maid to leave the room before responding. "Sophia," she said in a much firmer tone, "the Evertons are dear friends of mine, and I wouldn't insult them for anything. They only have one ball a Season, so this is your only chance."

Sophia wanted to point out that everyone seemed to be a "dear friend" of Aunt Nora's, but that would be impertinent. Sophia also wondered what her aunt meant by her "only chance." Her only chance for what? She assumed she must mean her only chance to attend a ball at the Evertons', but she didn't know why that could possibly matter to her. She knew that this pace would continue through the entire Season, and there would be many more balls.

The very thought of more balls made her feel dizzier and she closed and opened her eyes several times, hoping each time she popped her eyes open that the room would be still. Suddenly, she realized she wasn't staring at a *thing*; she was staring at a *man* who was staring back with a slightly puzzled expression. Sophia wondered how long she had been so impolitely staring at him. She felt a guilty expression cross her face and quickly looked away. "Couldn't we order the carriage now?" she quietly asked her aunt. "I am ever so tired."

Aunt Nora rolled her eyes to show annoyance, and Sophia was almost sorry she had asked. She sighed in relief, however, as Aunt Nora turned and led her toward the door.

Her sleepy mind took a few moments to realize that they weren't leaving. Instead, they had entered a long corridor. "Aunt Nora, where are we going? This isn't the way out."

Aunt Nora turned and led Sophia up a small flight of stairs. "No, it's not the way out, but our hostess informed me that they had a room where any lady needing rest could retire to for a time. You lie down for a few minutes, and I'm sure you'll feel rejuvenated."

Sophia waited to reply as they passed a maid who regarded her with a smug look—even the *servants* in London left her feeling inadequate. As the maid disappeared, Sophia lowered her voice as she said, "I really would just rather go. Couldn't I return home and have the carriage sent back for you?"

Aunt Nora didn't slow her step. She just pulled Sophia farther down the corridor. "Sophia, you aren't being very considerate. I'm disappointed to discover this selfishness in you." Sophia lowered her head and rubbed a hand over her eyes. She knew she was sometimes a bit selfish. Father had chided her about it occasionally, but she wished Aunt Nora hadn't discovered this. So much for her resolution to think of others first. She really must try harder.

Realizing that her best option was before her, Sophia looked up. "I'm sorry, Aunt Nora. Of course you should enjoy the ball. I'll rest here for a while." Aunt Nora had by this point opened the door to a room, and Sophia saw that it really was a very comfortable-looking sitting room. She turned back to her aunt before she could walk away. "You won't forget me, will you?" she asked. "I'm likely to fall asleep and not wake again till morning."

Aunt Nora smiled a genuine smile. "Of course I won't forget you. Have a nice rest, Sophia."

Sophia made her way to a sofa by the far window so she wouldn't disturb or be disturbed by any other tired young ladies who came in later. She lay down and closed her eyes but was surprised that sleep didn't come right away. Well, it was an unfamiliar room, and she was rather uncomfortable in her ball gown. She had almost fallen asleep standing up in the ballroom, but now her head throbbed and her eyes felt scratchy, and sleep was slow to come. She turned on her side, stared at a trunk that was in her line of vision, and counted the number of crisscrossing straps until sleep overtook her.

Four

Mr. Alexander Huntley *wondered why he had been of such* interest to the young lady across the room. She had been looking at him for several long moments, and he wondered if her thoughts were elsewhere. But when she finally seemed to realize that her prolonged gaze was noticed, she looked away with a guilty expression and soon after left the room with her chaperone. Probably she had heard the gossip about him from years ago and was judging and condemning him as all of London had. It shouldn't matter anymore, but still it hurt that he couldn't get away from his past.

Alex moved to a corner where a pillar blocked his view of most of the room, hoping to avoid any more critical stares. This was his first time back in five years, and the week he had already spent with the Evertons had been quite nice. Perhaps he was making too much of one judgmental stare from a stranger. Before returning to London, he had thought that everyone would treat him that way. But over the past week, he had been accepted and greeted in a friendly way by most of his old acquaintances. He wondered if perhaps he had been making too much of the past, but he knew that some in high society would never forget an indiscretion.

When he arrived a week ago, some of these very thoughts had plagued him. He only returned to London out of necessity. He didn't want to be in London; it brought back too many painful memories.

How different this arrival had been from the last time he came. Then he had arrived in his father's fine carriage with several servants in attendance. He had come with no other goal than to find entertainment. He had been a young man with thoughts only for the superficial.

For this trip to London, he arrived alone—in the same carriage, actually. But he was its driver, and it looked old and faded now. His goal was to complete his business and return home, hopefully avoiding all the entertainment that London was known for. As for his appearance . . . well, five years hadn't erased his youth completely, but he was sure that there were lines on his brow that had not been there on his last visit.

Five years—actually, it was almost five and a half years—made a very material difference in him. He had been so young and careless. Then everything in his life turned upside down upon his father's death. The difficult task of recovering his family estate seemed so daunting that he had wanted to give up, walk away from all his responsibilities, and never come back. But though the last five years had been hard, sometimes almost hopeless, he was grateful that he hadn't given up.

Alex still knew the streets of London well. Time hadn't erased his ability to navigate them, and he'd found his way easily to his destination. Lord Charles Everton was one of his very few friends who had remained faithful. The others had dropped

Alex's acquaintance when his fortunes had changed. They probably thought he would ask them for money, but he would never
accept money, let alone ask anyone for it. Even when he thought
he couldn't recover his family's estate, he still hadn't accepted the
money Charles had offered. That pride would have been his down-
fall, but good luck had saved him. His friendship with Charles was
as reliable as ever—something that wouldn't have been possible if
money had changed hands. And now Alex had the opportunity to
enjoy his friend's company as well as his hospitality. In fact a visit
had been long past due. Charles had been married for a year now,
and Alex still hadn't met Lady Everton.

Upon his arrival, he was shown in by the Evertons' butler, who
had obviously been expecting him because he led Alex directly to
Lord Everton's library.

"Hello, Charles," Alex greeted his old friend with a grin.
"Great to see you again."

"Alex, you're here already! Wonderful. I need your advice;
come and have a look at this map, will you? There's a fellow near
Colchester who's trying to sell me some land, and I'm not sure this
is an accurate survey. What d' you think?"

And just like that, Alex felt as if he and his friend had parted
just yesterday. He didn't possess that talent of easy camaraderie,
which was probably why he valued it so highly.

Having never been to Colchester, Alex didn't have much of
an opinion about the property in question, but they soon moved
on to other topics, mostly what all their common acquaintances
were doing now. Charles was convinced that everyone would be
as happy to see Alex as he had been and tried to persuade Alex to
visit their club. "Come, we'll have a little supper with Lucy. She'd
never forgive me otherwise. Then we'll head to the club, and I'll
reintroduce you to everyone. You're in for a great time."

"Actually, Charles," Alex hedged, "I'd much rather spend a
quiet evening in. I haven't even met Lucy yet. I'm sure we could

spend the whole evening talking and I won't have heard half of all that has happened since we parted."

But Charles wouldn't hear of it. From their regular correspondence, he understood Alex's situation. And if he had read between the lines, he knew more than Alex wanted him to know. Alex tried not to complain, but he had often written to his friend of the work and projects he was doing to recover his family home. Alex was sure that Charles thought he was a total recluse. He couldn't deny that these years spent away from polite society had been bereft of the typical fun of his youth. But there was a different kind of pleasure in hard work and restoration. Still, he never stepped back to enjoy the fruits of his hard work. Charles had invited him to stay with him repeatedly, but Alex never accepted his offer before. His constant focus was recovering what his father had lost. And even now, this trip was for business, not pleasure.

One of the reasons Alex avoided London so completely was because he couldn't afford its extravagance. Charles was possibly the only person with whom Alex could sacrifice his pride a little. "I've barely got my head above water, Charles," he admitted somberly. "There is no way I can spend an evening at the club gambling."

"Of course not, Alex. I won't lead you down any evil paths," he said exaggeratedly. "Tonight is just for reacquainting with good times. Besides, you've come to London to renegotiate mortgages with the bank. Doesn't that prove how far you've come?"

Alex still felt resistant but certainly was tempted. It would be nice to set financial worries aside, if just for an evening, and see how all his old friends were doing. The last two years had yielded especially fine crops. That, along with the return of tenants who had lost faith in his father, had created a substantial relief in his finances for Boxwell Court, his family estate. But Alex was so used to worrying about money and the livelihood of those beneath him that he couldn't relax. Rather, he pushed even harder to recover.

Through his constant vigilance, the future of Boxwell Court was looking quite promising, but it was difficult for him to let go of the safety of uninterrupted work. He felt if he put off his serious demeanor that somehow he would be exposed. But being in Charles's presence again gave him more confidence, and he felt that perhaps he had been worrying too much. A few more words of persuasion from Charles, and Alex's reluctance wore off.

Alex and Charles enjoyed an evening at the club, and it was just as great as Charles had said it would be.

After letting his guard down once, it was easier for Alex to relax and enjoy himself. In fact, staying with the Evertons for the week had been both busy and happy. But he never intended to relax enough to attend a ball. It had been Charles's lovely wife, Lucy, who had talked him into it. Although he wasn't completely happy about his choice, he couldn't help but smile a little as he thought about it.

He had overheard Lady Everton giving preparation instructions to a servant about a ball. That had stopped him in his tracks, and he'd waited until Lucy was disengaged.

"Did I hear you mention a ball just now, Lucy?" he asked.

"Alex! I, um . . . thought you had an appointment with your solicitor this morning." In the week that Alex had been there, he and Lucy had become good friends, but she looked upset to see him so unexpectedly.

"I'm just on my way now, but what is this about a ball? When is it exactly?"

Lucy looked a bit flustered but then boldly said, "Well, it's on Friday, actually."

Alex was sure he could conclude his business and be gone by then, and he breathed a sigh of relief. "You never mentioned it to me," he couldn't help saying. "Does Charles know he's hosting a ball on Friday, or will he be surprised too?"

Alex could tell what the answer was from Lucy's guilty

expression. He gave Lucy a look of mock reproach. "And here I've been trusting the pair of you like a lamb, never knowing you planned to feed me to the wolves."

Lucy looked slightly chagrined, but she rolled her eyes at the reference. "No one is going to eat you or tear you limb from limb. I promise you'll be quite safe. It's just a ball, Alex."

"Just a ball that I won't be here for," Alex stated with a slight shrug.

"You have to come!" Lucy protested. Then, as if making up her mind to be frank with him, she said, "Charles and I planned it especially so you would be here. Please don't tell Charles that you heard it from me. He knew you wouldn't want to attend, but he particularly asked me to postpone our annual ball so that you would be here for it." She paused before saying in a softer tone, "He worries about you, Alex. He's told me over and over how hard it's been for you since your father died, and he just wants you to enjoy life again."

Alex wasn't pleased to find himself an object of charity. He had spent five years trying to avoid pity of any kind. But he recognized the genuine friendship in their effort, so he chose his words carefully. "But, Lucy, I might be gone before the ball. I'm sure I can have everything settled by Thursday at the very latest."

Lucy gave a little shake of her head before he'd even finished speaking. "You shouldn't be so single-minded, Alex. Charles told me how . . . irresponsible you were when you were younger, and now you're nothing but responsible. You used to be all fun with no thought of work at all, and now you're the complete opposite—just work and nothing else! How about a little moderation?"

Alex was surprised at this assessment of his character. He'd never thought of it that way, but Lucy spoke the truth. He dedicated himself thoroughly to what he was doing in a very single-minded way. He wasn't sure he liked having this pointed out to him by someone so much younger than him, but Lucy seemed to be as opinionated as he was single-minded.

He sighed as he came to the inevitable conclusion: he didn't want to attend a ball, but it looked as though he would have to. Besides the need to create variety in his life, Alex also owed it to Charles for his steady friendship. So many others had abandoned him when he was left almost penniless. The one that he had tried to forget the most, of course, sprang to his mind, but he quickly pushed Miss Towler out of his thoughts and brought his gaze back to Lucy. She was demonstrating already that she was a true friend. And, of course, Charles was a friend for life, not just for the good times. And with friends like that, the least he could do was accept an invitation to their ball and attend with good grace. He owed them much more than that.

"All right, Lucy. A little moderation is just what I need," he said with a friendly smile. "I won't let Charles know that I know. We'll let him think he's tricked me into attending."

"Thank you, Alex," Lucy answered with conspiratorial grin. "You won't regret it." Then she set to work once again with her preparations, and Alex, smile still on his face, made his way to Chapel Street for his appointment.

Standing now in the corner of the Evertons' ballroom, Alex was almost sorry that he hadn't come to London sooner. Not because he was enjoying the ball, but because Charles and Lucy were the kind of invaluable friends that he didn't want to lose.

Alex stepped out from behind the pillar and looked around for them now. They were an elegant pair, and even in a ballroom they stood out. He found Lucy by the hue of her blue dress, and when he saw that she and Charles weren't looking his way, he quietly left the ballroom. He had done his duty long enough. He had danced with Lucy and then with three or four other young ladies. He had chatted with gentlemen that he hadn't seen in several years. He had been unfailingly polite throughout the whole evening, even when that unfamiliar young lady had stared at him in that critical way.

It had been a little over five years since he'd last attended a ball, and besides the fact that he knew fewer people in the room, nothing had changed. Well, that wasn't true—he had changed. Thinking back to his youth, he remembered that in the past he would have danced every dance with only the most beautiful young ladies in the room, flirting the whole time. Then he would have left the ball and gone to the club, where he would have squandered money and time with undeserving friends.

He was so serious these days that he was sure he would be out of place at a ball, but that hadn't been the case. He'd made an effort to enjoy himself, and it had worked. He was discovering that Lucy was right: he needed moderation. Putting his worries aside and enjoying the ball had been an effort, though, and he would gladly wait awhile before attending another. Besides, he wasn't looking for a wife, so a ball was of little use to him.

Alex entered his room, removed his jacket and cravat, and breathed a sigh in relaxation. He was grateful to Charles and Lucy. They had forced this social situation on him, and he was pleased they had. It felt good, he realized, and he felt more alive again. Maybe if the next five years went well, he wouldn't have to be forced back into society.

Alex pulled off his boots, then picked up his candle and looked around the room for where he had left his book. That was when he saw her. A young lady—either asleep or dead—was on his sofa! He almost dropped the candle, but he quickly steadied it instead and rushed over. Her skin was warm, but it seemed as if she wasn't breathing. He forced himself to be calm as he checked again and realized that she was breathing, just very slowly and deeply. He sat down hard on the floor and leaned his head back against the sofa. Then he took his own deep breath in an effort to calm his racing heart. She was alive, thank goodness! She was just sleeping.

How strange that a young lady was asleep in his room . . . his eyes widened, and his heart began racing again. He needed to get her out of here. Now!

He quickly turned around and tried to gently speak to her and shake her shoulder. Several increasingly more frantic pleas of "Miss, you need to wake up!" produced no results. So he lifted her up to a sitting position, but still she wouldn't regain consciousness. He sat down next to her and pulled her arm around his shoulder, ready to stand up, which would hopefully rouse her enough to walk, and that was when he heard a commotion from the hall and then a knock on his door. He barely had time to blurt out, "One moment, please!" before several matronly women barged in.

Five

Sophia was being called from a very deep sleep back to reality, and it was a slow journey. She couldn't remember where she was. The time and day were both a mystery that her mind was trying to solve. And why was she waking up to chaotic conversation all around her? She was sitting up and leaning against someone, but she must have been pulled to that position. Still trying to open her eyes, she finally looked up to see who was tugging on her arm and saw Aunt Nora. Oh yes, they had been at a ball . . . the Evertons' ball . . . and she had fallen asleep in the sitting room set aside for young ladies. Aunt Nora was there, so it must be time to go. Several other ladies were in the room, and they all seemed to be talking over one another. Sophia blinked several times and lifted her head off the firm shoulder it was resting on. She let her aunt pull her up off the sofa. Aunt Nora put her arm around Sophia, who was just conscious enough to be surprised at the protective embrace. She thought she heard a man's voice, which couldn't be right. It was then she started paying attention to the words that were being spoken.

"I'll expect you tomorrow at the very latest!" Aunt Nora was saying.

Another woman's voice said, "Of course he'll have to right this wrong immediately! Oh, Lady Bloomfield, how distraught you must be . . ."

Sophia was still wrapped in confusion. She wanted to lift her head and ask Aunt Nora what had happened, but her head was being pressed into Aunt Nora's shoulder.

Then she *did* hear a man's voice, which quite surprised her. "This is all a misunderstanding, ladies. Please, just be calm. I did not know the young lady was in my room!"

Before he even finished he was interrupted. "This isn't a misunderstanding. It's a complete breach of honor!" and then another voice said, "You will have to make a match now to save this poor girl!"

Sophia was becoming more awake but wished she wasn't. She saw the man stand up from the sofa where she had just been sleeping and begin to pace. She started to feel a sick dread in her stomach, which was quickly driving the sleepiness away. With some effort, she pulled back from Aunt Nora's embrace and said, "Aunt, can we leave now? I'm quite ready to go if you are."

"Oh, my poor niece! Of course, let's get you home." Then, pulling Sophia back in to the protective hold, Aunt Nora said, "And, Mr. Huntley, we will discuss the repercussions of this tomorrow!" With that, Aunt Nora marched from the room, which was rather awkward for Sophia, who was still tucked under her arm.

Alex watched them leave in silent fury. The scene was just as awful as he had feared it would be. He had done his best to talk himself out of the situation, but no one would let him get a word in. The women had fluttered around him with a noise that reminded him quite clearly of seagulls fighting over a morsel of food. The three of them had made it abundantly clear that he had dishonored the girl and would have to marry her immediately. Trying to placate them only seemed to agitate them more. At some point, the young lady had *finally* woken up. She had asked to leave, and as she did, her gaze briefly landed on Alex, and he realized he had noticed her earlier this evening.

She was the very same young lady who had stared at him from across the room.

Suspicious of the situation, he stopped talking and observed the women. The aunt, whom he believed was Lady Bloomfield, had an malicious gleam in her eye. And the girl, her "poor niece," wouldn't lift her eyes again. They left the room in righteous indignation. Alex felt his defensiveness turn to anger as he realized he had been caught in a trap!

Six

"Aunt Nora, what has happened? Why are you so distressed? And who was that man?" Sophia had at least ten more questions, but she stopped to hear her aunt's answer. But Aunt Nora just shushed her as their wraps were brought to them and their carriage was sent for.

Sophia was becoming more and more agitated. Trying to piece the bits of conversation together that she had heard—well, she was finding it difficult to breathe.

Lady Everton came rushing into the hall as they waited.

Sophia hadn't paid much attention before, but now she noticed how young Lady Everton looked. She wondered if someone not much older than she was could fix whatever was so suddenly going horribly wrong. Sophia watched as Lady Everton clasped Aunt Nora's hand, concern evident in her manner. Sophia moved closer so she could hear what she was saying. ". . . just heard what has happened, but I'm sure it's all just an innocent mistake."

Her aunt's reply wasn't difficult to hear. Although her aunt talked to Lady Everton in a voice that was trying to be quiet, somehow it carried through the entry hall so that everyone standing nearby could hear.

"I am just shocked that this could have happened, Lady Everton! That one of your guests would behave in such a way . . . well, you can see I'm almost too overcome to even speak!" Sophia was beginning to wish that were true. The distress in her aunt's voice was drawing attention; others were paying heed to what was being said. Sophia still wasn't perfectly certain what had happened while she slept, but she was sure that it was a private matter.

"My niece, who is in the first weeks of her first Season, now has everything snatched away from her! She'll have to marry Mr. Huntley immediately to save her poor name. I am sure that my sister is turning in her grave at this poor treatment of her only daughter."

Sophia didn't even realize her mouth hung open in shock. "Marry . . . that man in the room? That . . . Mr. Huntley?" As her confusion cleared, she looked up and felt her face flame with embarrassment. Her mumbled questions were meant for her aunt, but there were probably a dozen other people in the room. Some were servants, but some were obviously guests, and they were all looking at her with sympathy, incredulity, or disdain.

Sophia wished to sink into the floor. The ability to faint suddenly seemed like an enviable talent. If only she had learned how! But she just stood there, as miserable as she could ever remember being, while her aunt spoke in irate tones and Lady Everton tried to soothe.

The reality of her situation hit her as she listened to her aunt. All her questions were answered. She had been alone with a man in his chambers! It didn't seem to matter to anyone that she had been asleep. It was quite apparent that her reputation was ruined and marriage was now expected—not just expected, but required.

Finally their carriage arrived. The desire to run away from this humiliating experience was almost overwhelming. Lady Everton delayed them a bit longer as she tried one last time to convince Aunt Nora that the situation was not so dire as it seemed. "Lady Bloomfield, I have the utmost trust and respect for Mr. Huntley. He has been a close friend of Lord Everton's for years. I can assure you most confidently that he had no designs on Miss Spencer. Perhaps we can get to the bottom of this misunderstanding and everything could be made right."

Sophia clung to that small bit of hope but was devastated again as Aunt Nora rejected it. "You may trust Mr. Huntley, Lady Everton, but I do not." Aunt Nora raised her eyebrows in a challenging look. "Do you not remember all that happened several years ago? Why, it's a well-known fact that he tried to elope with Harriet Towler just to get his hands on her fortune. Harriet was only saved because she admitted their plans to her father, who put a stop to it all."

Sophia watched Lady Everton's reaction as her aunt retold the rumor. It was obvious that Lady Everton knew about it, but she didn't have any defense of her friend's actions. "Now it seems my niece has been caught in his next trap. And this time there is no way out! She'll have to marry him!"

With that, Sophia was pulled along in her aunt's wake to their awaiting carriage. She was conscious of being watched, but she resisted the temptation to look behind her. What a spectacle they had been!

Sophia's tears came as soon as the carriage door was closed. Aunt Nora didn't try to comfort her. She was probably still too upset herself. Sophia didn't even look up; she just sobbed as quietly as she could into her hands while the carriage jolted forward and carried them home. It was a short journey back, and when they reached home, Sophia fled to her room. She didn't even call her maid. She just lay on her bed and cried at her awful predicament.

Finally, she prepared herself for bed. She lit a candle and undressed. Then she pulled at the pins in her hair until it all came down. She climbed back into bed, anxious for oblivion. Crying had exhausted her, and she felt more tired than before. However, for the second time that night, she couldn't fall asleep, even though she had never been so desperate for it in her life.

Seven

When Sophia woke up the next day, it took only a few moments of consciousness before she remembered the events of the previous evening and groaned out loud.

Immediately, she pictured all the censorious looks that had been cast her way last night. With a sinking feeling in the pit of her stomach, Sophia thought about the escalating reactions as everyone realized what had happened. She had been pulled away from the ball in absolute shame, with everyone staring at her and judging her. Sophia felt guilty but tried to push that feeling aside—those people didn't know that she hadn't done anything wrong. Everyone thought she was wicked, but they didn't know the truth: it had all been an accident.

She had never been in a fix quite like this before. This was definitely the worst ever, worse even than the time she had tried to be a peacemaker when her governess had argued with Mrs. Jenkins, the shopkeeper. Sophia had totally botched the job.

She could no longer remember what their argument had been about, but she did remember how each woman had insisted that she was right. She had told each of them separately that the other was ready to admit she was wrong and beg forgiveness. When they realized they'd been had, all their anger transferred to Sophia, and she had spent most of that afternoon hiding in Lord Fitzgerald's oak tree by the river.

Somehow, she didn't think her problems would disappear today if she hid in a tree. Reluctantly she called her maid, who came in with a hesitant "good afternoon, miss." Sophia covered her face with her hands; it was obvious the servants already knew her predicament. Then she looked up with a puzzled expression. "Did you say 'good afternoon,' Ellie?"

"Yes, miss. It's past two now." She continued to give Sophia a wary look, wondering if this news was somehow upsetting.

Sophia groaned again. She really shouldn't have let the day get away from her. She needed to get up and face this problem head-on. How would she ever find a way out of this predicament by sleeping?

She sent Ellie to fetch her a tray—she was *starving*—and then used Ellie's help to quickly get dressed in between bites. Once she was presentable, Sophia went in search of her aunt. It was time to make some explanations so that this misunderstanding could be put behind them.

She found her aunt in the parlor. "Hello, Sophia," Aunt Nora greeted her. "You've missed your fiancé. He came to call while you were sleeping."

Several responses sprang to mind: *I don't have a fiancé!* And, *Why didn't you wake me?* And even, *There is something green caught between your teeth, Aunt Nora.* But all of Sophia's breath had left her in a surprised exhale.

Aunt Nora continued speaking in a calm, satisfied voice as if she were discussing the pleasant weather. "Mr. Huntley and I worked out all the details for the wedding, which will be the day after tomorrow. Lord Everton is helping him procure a special license so you won't have to wait. Mr. Huntley wanted to speak with you as well, but I wouldn't disturb you for the world, and I told him so. I informed him that if he insisted on speaking with you, he would have to return tomorrow."

Sophia sat down hard on the sofa and looked at her aunt in distress. "This has gone too far! Oh, Aunt Nora, why couldn't you explain that I must have fallen asleep in his room by mistake?" Without waiting for a reply, Sophia continued, "Everyone needs to know that it was an innocent mistake. Couldn't we go today, right now, and explain to Lord and Lady Everton, and to Mr. Huntley too, that I didn't mean to fall asleep there?"

Aunt Nora looked at Sophia with a look of rueful sympathy. "Sophia, when I came to find you, Mrs. Jones and Lady Barrett were both with me. And you and Mr. Huntley were in quite an intimate pose when we came upon you."

Sophia's head reared back slightly at that. She had been asleep. The first thing she remembered from last night was her aunt pulling her up. Slowly the realization dawned that she had been sitting on the sofa, leaning against someone . . . apparently Mr. Huntley. This was awful! Sophia felt her face flame as she thought about how it must have looked.

Pushing that thought aside, she said, "You know what I think, Aunt Nora? We must have somehow gone to the wrong sitting room last night. I'm sure if we explained to Lord and Lady Everton and Mr. Huntley that it was an honest mistake, they wouldn't hold it against us. We'll have to tell Mrs. Jones and Lady Barrett too, and then, of course, anyone else who might have inadvertently heard . . ." Sophia's voice trailed off as she realized it would be a large task to clear her name.

Aunt Nora sighed and spoke as if she were explaining a difficult concept to a very small child. "Sophia, in refined society, there are rules, and when those rules are broken, there are consequences."

Sophia was feeling a bit desperate. "May I please just speak to Mr. Huntley? When he calls tomorrow, I'll explain everything then. I'm sure he'll be as relieved as I will be to call off this whole wedding!"

Again Aunt Nora looked at Sophia in a condescending way. "Mr. Huntley is a well-known fortune hunter, Sophia. He probably planned this whole thing to get at your inheritance. All he needed was to find a naïve young miss with loads of money and then be caught alone with her." Aunt Nora shrugged her shoulders in helplessness. "He'll be the least likely person to want to call off the wedding."

Sophia slumped back against the sofa. She knew her aunt was right. When Aunt Nora had reminded Lady Everton of Mr. Huntley's past last night, there had been no denial. Apparently he had tried to elope with a young lady just to get her fortune. That plan hadn't worked, but this one had. He must have arranged it all somehow.

Sophia stood up and paced. If Mr. Huntley had truly planned the incident, then it would be much harder to undo what had been done. Her only hope had been that he was as dismayed at what had happened as she was, and then together they could have explained everything away. Now what was she going to do? How could she possibly escape this situation if Mr. Huntley had orchestrated the whole thing?

"I've canceled our engagements for today and tomorrow," Aunt Nora said, interrupting her thinking. "I sent notes to each hostess saying that you were unwell. I doubt they'll believe that; by now they will all have heard of the scandal." Shaking her head gently, she made a small tsk-tsk sound and said, "Such a shame." As if missing a rout and cancelling a card party were the biggest regrets of the whole incident!

Sophia stopped her pacing and observed her aunt, who was working on an embroidery project that claimed her attention, so she didn't notice Sophia's stare. Her aunt's regretful tone some-how didn't match her expression. Aunt Nora seemed to care about the superficial so much more than the things that really mattered. Sophia was realizing that her aunt was a person whose feelings didn't run deep. When she had arrived, her expectations had been for a deep love to form between herself and her aunt. She had been so ready to have a mother figure to look up to and love. She had felt close to her aunt over the last few weeks, but it was obviously not a strong bond, because it seemed to be crumbling apart. It felt as though her aunt had abandoned her at the first sign of trouble, and Sophia felt completely alone in this dilemma.

From the moment they met, Sophia tried to emulate her sophisticated aunt. But now observing her, Sophia wondered if she had made a mistake. Why would she want to be like this woman, who only cared about how she appeared to others?

In annoyance, Sophia turned to leave the room. Before she reached the door, she turned back and said, "Aunt, you have something green caught between your teeth." Then she indicated which teeth she meant by pointing at her own.

Sophia smiled at her aunt's annoyed discomfiture. Then she turned again and left.

Eight

Mr. Huntley arrived the next morning, and Sophia was ready. She had spent a lot of time coming up with several valid reasons to cancel the upcoming nuptials. If only she could convince Mr. Huntley!

He was shown into the drawing room, where Sophia and Aunt Nora were sitting in expectation of his arrival.

Sophia hadn't actually gotten a good look at Mr. Huntley, and she couldn't quite remember what he looked like. All she had seen of him that night was dark brown hair and a navy coat.

As he entered the room, she discreetly took a mental inventory of the rest of his appearance. She was surprised to notice how tall he was; she hadn't remembered having to look up into his eyes. His hair was definitely brown, but lighter than she'd thought, perhaps because the room the other night had been so dark. He was actually quite handsome. But as Sophia looked at his eyes—noting as she did that they were blue—she noticed his stern expression. Sophia felt as though she had accidentally done something wrong by looking him over.

After he gave a brief bow as a greeting, they all sat down.

"Mr. Huntley," Aunt Nora greeted, "you are most prompt this morning." Which could have been a compliment, but her aunt's tone made sure it wasn't.

He didn't reply; he just looked back and forth between Sophia and her aunt for several long seconds.

"Sophia was *distraught* that she missed you yesterday, weren't you, Sophia?" Aunt Nora said, making another effort at conversation. Before Sophia could confirm or deny being distraught yesterday—which she had been, but not for the reason Aunt Nora's tone implied—her aunt kept speaking. "I've invited several close friends to attend the wedding ceremony tomorrow, and they all sent back replies saying they wouldn't miss it. I hope there weren't any delays on your part, Mr. Huntley, in obtaining the license?" This time her aunt did pause for a reply.

"No delays at all, Lady Bloomfield," was Mr. Huntley's civil response.

"And did you arrange everything with the vicar at St. Luke's?" she asked.

"Yes, Lady Bloomfield. All is set for tomorrow's ceremony at ten in the morning," he replied evenly.

Sophia's eyes widened, and her anxiety grew as her aunt asked several more detailed questions about tomorrow's event while Mr. Huntley politely replied. Everything was planned and ready. It felt as if there were too many wheels in motion. There was no way she could stop this! Taking a deep breath, she tried to calm down. She might not persuade Mr. Huntley and her aunt out of this predicament, but she was at least going to try.

"Mr. Huntley," she began at the first pause from her aunt, "do you not feel that this is all a bit sudden?" She saw his eyebrows go up in surprise but hurried on before she lost her nerve. "We don't know each other at all. Perhaps we could put the wedding off for a few weeks. We could . . ." Sophia hesitated as she tried to phrase her thoughts carefully into words. ". . . learn more about each other." This wasn't Sophia's plan at all— she had no desire to learn more about Mr. Huntley. The only plans she had come up with so far were very far-fetched schemes. But surely with more time, *something* would come to her.

Mr. Huntley didn't answer right away. Instead, he scrutinized her for a few moments, and Sophia felt herself grow self-conscious and blush, but she didn't look away. This was too important. He was looking at her so intently, as if trying to peer into her soul.

His delay in answering Sophia's request gave her aunt the opportunity to jump in. "Sophia, of all the things to ask! The wedding cannot be delayed. Why, the only reason it is so soon is for your benefit. Surely you realize that this is all to save your reputation."

Mr. Huntley watched the interaction closely, looking back and forth between the two of them as her aunt spoke. His eyes narrowed slightly in what looked like suspicion. "Miss Spencer, I think Lady Bloomfield is right. The wedding must take place, no matter what. Whether it is tomorrow or in a month's time is of no significance to me."

Sophia wondered if this were true. If Mr. Huntley wanted her inheritance so badly, surely he would want to marry her quickly to secure it. The thought hardly occurred to her before he continued, "However, in order to do as little damage to your reputation as possible, the sooner we marry, the better." Mr. Huntley's voice had a ring of finality that caused a flutter of anxiety to run through Sophia. But she wasn't ready to give up.

"Mr. Huntley, I would really feel so much better if my father could attend the ceremony." Her voice wasn't completely steady; this reason for a delay was entirely true. "Surely he needs to be there to give his permission, at the least."

Again, her aunt answered before Mr. Huntley could. "Sophia, you have been under my care while you've been in London, and I, of course, sanction the wedding. Besides, you are old enough to marry without consent; there is no reason to wait for your father."

Mr. Huntley nodded his agreement as he stood to take his leave. Sophia and her aunt stood too. It was wholly out of instinct that Sophia grabbed Mr. Huntley's arm. She wanted to stop him from leaving until she could convince him to stop the wedding, but whatever she was about to say flew out of her mind as soon as she touched him. She wasn't *really* touching him, though—just his arm encased in his coat. He felt so strong and solid. That strength felt so real, and Sophia was sure that if she could get him on her side, they could accomplish anything—even stop this ridiculous wedding. She gazed into his icy-blue eyes to implore him one more time. He looked rather pointedly at her, then to her hand on his arm, and back at her again. Sophia grew embarrassed. She snatched her hand away and shook it a little as though his gaze had caused it pain. Feeling completely awkward, she clasped her hands behind her back, gave a slight curtsy, and mumbled, "Good day to you, Mr. Huntley."

"Miss Spencer, Lady Bloomfield." Mr. Huntley nodded to them both in farewell and left the room.

Sophia excused herself immediately. The last thing she wanted was to hear her aunt's opinion on what had just transpired. She spent several hours in her room, breaking down in tears every so often and thinking of ways to cancel the wedding. Most of them involved the accidental death of Mr. Huntley, her aunt, herself, or even the vicar, so it was unlikely that any of them would happen. She gradually accepted the fact that this was her fate. There didn't seem to be any way out of the predicament she had landed in. It was a difficult thing to accept.

Before coming to London, Sophia had dreamed of a fairy tale romance, like her parents had had. They had gone against the wishes of her mother's family and married for love. Her mother had been gone more than fifteen years and her father had never remarried, even though there had been no lack of opportunities for him. Sophia had taken these basic facts about her parents and romanticized them further, until their true love was the epitome of all she wanted in this life. She had come to London determined to settle for nothing less. How quickly that ideal had crumbled to pieces.

She was suddenly terribly homesick. She had hardly spared a thought for home. Except a few hurried letters scrawled to her father, she had been too busy to even miss him. Oh, but she missed him now. What would he say when he heard about these dreadful events? The next time she saw him, she would be Mrs. Huntley! After that thought occurred to her, she tried again to figure out a way to stop it all. But she came to all the same conclusions.

She also thought about Mr. Huntley's involvement in the whole affair. Her aunt had said that Mr. Huntley was a fortune hunter who must have planned the whole thing. But reflecting on the events that led up to them being found together, she realized that it couldn't be true. Before the Evertons' ball, she had never even seen him. She was the one who had been tired, and her aunt had led her to the room where she could rest. He couldn't have planned those events. Mr. Huntley may be a fortune hunter, but he hadn't planned this incident. It must have truly been an accident.

Still, things had worked out well for him. With hardly any effort, he was acquiring a wife with money—how much money she still wasn't sure. She had yet to meet with Mr. Wilson. That would have to wait, but surely her grandmother's investments would come to several thousand pounds. It was strange that Mr. Huntley didn't seem happier about the whole situation. Maybe that wasn't enough for a fortune hunter; perhaps he had set his sights much higher than her meager inheritance.

For the first time since the ball, instead of thinking how she was the one suffering from a grave injustice, she tried to imagine how Mr. Huntley must feel about it. He had shown almost no emotion—just succinct politeness—in front of Sophia. Was he pleased but hiding it? Was he distressed but hiding it? She knew too little about him to even guess the answers to these questions. Perhaps, in time, they would come to know each other well enough that she could ask him. One thing was certain, however: no matter how either of them was feeling, the result was the same—they were getting married tomorrow.

Nine

*A*lex left Lady Bloomfield's home with his anger simmering beneath the surface—but that was where his anger would have to remain. In order to recover any respectability, he would have to *act* respectably. It wasn't easy, though. From the moment he realized that he had walked into a snare, he had been furious. This is what came from letting his guard down and enjoying himself. He should have concentrated on his business and left London as soon as he could. His regrets weren't helping matters. He couldn't change what had happened. All he could do was deal with the situation at hand.

Yesterday had been awful. Charles and Lucy felt terrible, taking all the blame on themselves because it had occurred at their ball. They had apologized repeatedly and were determined to find out how Miss Spencer had ended up in his room. An investigation was underway in their house at that moment. All the servants were being questioned, specifically as to whether they'd seen anything suspicious. Alex felt it was a waste of time. He knew exactly how it had happened: Lady Bloomfield and Miss Spencer had plotted it all.

Actually, he wasn't completely sure of Miss Spencer's involvement anymore. Watching her interact with her aunt left him with doubts about her contribution to the plot. Perhaps Miss Spencer was simply a talented actress. The fact that she had been staring across the room at him at the ball made him think that she had been watching him like a hunter watches prey. Most likely her resistance to the marriage was a new plot of her own to manipulate him later on.

It didn't really matter whether she was a scheming conniver or an innocent fool. Alex didn't want to marry her either way. He didn't want to get married at all.

If he had his desire, it would be several years at least before he even looked for a wife. By then he would choose much more carefully than when he had rashly asked Miss Towler to marry him. They had been merely friends who flirted together, part of a group of the young and careless. When word reached Alex in London that his father had died and the creditors were closing in fast, he proposed to Harriet Towler, thinking that the artificial bond they had was real. And, yes, he admitted to himself, the fact that she was rich had been an incentive.

She had said yes, but obviously it was just being caught up in the moment, because before their planned elopement could take place, she had told everything to her father, who put a stop to it all. Very publicly, in fact. Alex's humiliation was complete.

Alex had returned home in disgrace to find servants, tenants, and the local village—all of whom had been dependent on his family for generations—anxiously waiting for him to take over and lead them. Alex had dreaded the responsibility before his father had squandered so much, and after, it seemed impossible. With his two older sisters already married and moved away and his mother staying with one of them, Alex had returned alone to a cavernous house with responsibility threatening to smother him. He had seriously contemplated just giving everything up and walking away. Boxwell Court was beautiful and vast, and his family had resided there for almost four hundred years. But, as his father's accountant had told Alex as he packed his things, it was so encumbered by debt that it might take more than one lifetime to recover.

Alex realized these negative memories weren't helping his mood one bit. Despite all the odds, he had made substantial progress in recovering Boxwell Court. What really made him angry was that all his hard work would be wasted on a manipulative wife. He wanted to be in a perpetually black mood, but with Charles and Lucy he felt obligated to hide it; they felt guilty enough already. So he buried his negative thoughts and feelings and returned to Grosvenor Street.

Ten

*A*unt *Nora arrived with Ellie the next morning to help Sophia* dress. Ellie was quick to follow all of Aunt Nora's orders and pulled out a deep blue gown from Sophia's wardrobe.

"Ah, yes. This is the one you should be married in, Sophia. It's by far the most elegant of all your new gowns."

But for the first time since arriving in London, Sophia asserted herself. "No. That one is too heavy, and it's warm today. I want to wear my lavender gown." Sophia saw a look of amusement cross her aunt's features and knew that Aunt Nora thought she was behaving like a petulant child, but at least Sophia got her way. The lavender gown was much simpler and lighter, with a wide white satin ribbon tied around her waist and a collar of the same white ribbon at her neck.

Ellie procured the gown and then helped Sophia dress. She carefully and artfully arranged Sophia's hair exactly as her aunt instructed. And through it all, Aunt Nora gave the usual backward compliments that Sophia had come to expect from her aunt. She had grown used to feeling a little inferior and out of place after her aunt's scrutiny, but today she was a bit wizened to her aunt's character, so she just felt irritated.

"You know, I think you were right to choose the lavender gown, Sophia. It really is sweet, don't you think? Not what one would wear to impress, of course, but still . . . very sweet." Then it was, "I can never decide if your hair is nearer to blonde or brown. Still, Ellie has arranged it beautifully. It really looks quite bridal." And later, "I had hoped to fatten you up a bit during your stay. Shame there's no time for that now. Oh well, I'm sure you'll do . . ."

Sophia honestly didn't care how she looked, but her aunt's manners were so provoking.

Two maids came to the room while Ellie was preparing Sophia. One of them set down Sophia's breakfast tray, and then both began following her aunt's instructions for packing Sophia's things. Of course, all her new things wouldn't fit in the one trunk Sophia had brought with her from Tissington, but Aunt Nora promised to have all her new things sent along later. Sophia didn't touch her breakfast tray. She couldn't possibly eat at a time like this. Far too soon, Sophia was ready to go, and her aunt led her to the carriage.

A very short ride later, Sophia found herself disembarking at St. Luke's. Her feet didn't seem to want to move, but Aunt Nora pulled her along into the church. Once inside, her eyes immediately found Mr. Huntley. He was speaking with Lord and Lady Everton and the vicar, but the conversation halted as she and her aunt came in.

Her eyes locked with his as she and her aunt approached the group. Sophia wrapped her arms around herself to ward off the chill she felt as their footsteps echoed hollowly against the cold stone. Subdued greetings were exchanged by all except her aunt, who seemed to view this wedding as a happy event. The Evertons and the vicar moved to the front of the church as she and her aunt continued speaking with Mr. Huntley.

"Well, Mr. Huntley, here is your blushing bride. She was so excited this morning that she didn't touch her breakfast." Aunt Nora's tone made Sophia feel mocked. She slumped her shoulders and rolled her eyes in a resigned way. Mr. Huntley, watching her, narrowed his eyes in a speculative glance. Sophia didn't bother to say anything. How could she contradict her aunt without sounding ridiculous? Besides, her aunt continued speaking in the same vein, and Sophia didn't have a chance to interject. She dared another glance at Mr. Huntley and saw he was annoyed as well—but he was looking right at her, as if she were the one who annoyed him.

Sophia didn't think she could marry him while he was looking at her like that. She had to try something. "Er . . . Mr. Huntley," she began, interrupting her aunt midspeech, "could I speak to you a moment?"

Mr. Huntley looked down at her with an impatient look. "We are speaking, Miss Spencer."

Mr. Huntley's annoyance, and the fact that he wasn't trying to hide it, unnerved her, and she stammered her request. "Yes . . . of course, I . . . well, I'd like to, er . . . discuss something with you . . ." Sophia's eyes shifted to her aunt, then back to Mr. Huntley's cravat, and she cleared her throat nervously. "Maybe we could step outside for a moment?" She was eager to have at least one conversation with her future husband in private without her aunt adding some hidden layer of meaning to everything she said or answering Sophia's questions before Mr. Huntley could himself, as had happened the day before.

"Very well, Miss Spencer." And he lifted an impatient hand toward the door, gesturing for her to precede him. Leaving her aunt behind, Sophia led the way out of the building.

"Mr. Huntley," Sophia said as soon as they reached the outer door of the church, "I've been anxious to apologize for what happened. It was an accident, I assure you. I had no idea that this would be the consequence for falling asleep at a ball." Now that Sophia had begun speaking of it, the unfairness of their predicament really seemed too much. How could such a trivial thing result in a marriage? "I don't know a thing about you, and we're about to be married!" she said, stating the obvious, but Mr. Huntley didn't comment. She glanced up, and he was looking at her coldly. She couldn't read his emotions; she didn't know him well enough to interpret his stare. His look wasn't one of understanding or forgiveness, that was certain.

Sophia turned toward the side of the building to walk along the path that wound past the headstones. She was feeling more uneasy with each passing moment she spent with her future husband. How could they possibly walk back into that church and promise their lives to each other? Her insides fluttered at the thought, and she knew she had to connect to this man . . . somehow. But she had no experience breaking down walls of stony anger. She ineptly searched for words that would convey how she felt.

"I'm nervous . . . ," she heard herself saying, "about the future, er, the future for us together." She stammered on, "How will we manage? I realize that this is not what either of us wanted. I suppose . . . or rather, I was wondering if everything is going to be all right."

When Mr. Huntley didn't answer again, she felt even more distant from him than before. She couldn't look up to meet his gaze. As she waited for reassurance, Sophia stared at the tips of her slippers that poked out from under her wedding dress with each step.

Mr. Huntley still didn't say anything, so she clarified, "Is marriage really the best decision for us?"

Mr. Huntley stopped, and Sophia paused too. She was hoping for some calm words of reassurance. She needed to *feel* reassured to walk back into that church and say her vows. As she met his expression, however, she was surprised to see frustration and anger across his features. He had been so carefully calm discussing the details of the wedding in the parlor with her aunt. His politeness had never faltered on the surface. He had shown only polite reserve as he spoke agreeable words. Now, though, he didn't seem to be repressing any feelings. He crossed his arms and narrowed his eyes in anger.

"'Decision,' Miss Spencer?" he asked, shaking his head gently with an incredulous look. "'Decision,'" he repeated. His tone of voice indicating he thought she had no intelligence whatsoever. "There is no *decision* anymore. Any choice we had was taken from us when you and I were found together in my room." He included himself in the statement, but it was obvious that he considered her to be the one at fault. Sophia sucked in a breath to defend herself. She had been aching to explain, but before she could speak, he continued angrily, "The only choice we have now is to be married. The only option now is to tie our lives together and hope that at length we can tolerate one another. How I'm ever going to tolerate such a weak character as yours is beyond me. To let your aunt completely control you as she does—why, if you had any backbone at all, we wouldn't be in this predicament!"

Now that he had let his anger loose, it seemed to become more potent every moment. His anger frightened Sophia, and she shrank back against the words.

"You ask if everything will be all right? No, it won't. It will be all wrong. I didn't ask for this, but marriage is the only *decision*," he mocked, "that we can make now. We don't have any other choice. We either get married, or your reputation is ruined!" He turned and stalked back to the church.

Sophia couldn't help the tears that came then. She stumbled a few paces to a low stone bench, sat down with her face buried in her hands, and cried. She had never provoked anger like that in anyone before. Her father had only ever reprimanded her in the gentlest way, and only on rare occasions. Is this what marriage to Mr. Huntley would be like? Would he either be coldly polite or hatefully angry? How would she ever survive such environment? Now that she understood that Mr. Huntley blamed her for the whole thing, she knew he was right: it would be a miracle if they ever learned to tolerate each other. She knew it would be an uphill battle to even desire to be in his presence again. She saw her dream of marrying and creating a happy family with a loving husband disappearing.

Sophia thought about her near-perfect childhood. All her needs had been met, and many of her wants. She had a loving father, who still looked at her as though she made the sun rise each day. She had wanted only for a mother. Well, she had also wanted brothers and sisters, but as she got older and began helping her father by minding young children while he doctored them she changed her mind. They were always crying inconsolably and dripping from their noses and eyes so that she didn't want to touch them. Caring for them left her exhausted. It was always a relief to finally leave. Sophia became content without siblings of her own. But for some reason, those times helping her father had never changed the desire in her to be a mother herself. She knew she would be such a wonderful mother that her children would never cry or even be ill.

She sniffed, and a watery chuckle came through her tears as she remembered how unreasonable her assumptions had been. Of course she knew that all children became ill and cried quite a lot. She wanted them anyway, enough children that they would never feel alone. And then the tears started fresh again. No happy family with mischievous brothers and imaginative sisters would ever come to be if she married Mr. Huntley. But what choice did she have? He had stated it too clearly for doubt: they had to be married, or her reputation was ruined.

Sophia heard her name being called in a rather sharp tone of voice. Her aunt came around the corner of the church, looking for her. "Sophia! They are ready to begin. You have to come, now!" Sophia looked up at Aunt Nora, who was close enough to see the tears on her cheeks and sighed in exasperation. Pulling out a handkerchief, she admonished, "Please dry your face. Do you want to embarrass me? Several of my friends are here this morning to see you married as a favor to me, so that you won't have to say your vows in an empty church. Could you at least look like a bride?"

"But, Aunt Nora, I don't want to marry him! He's not kind at all! Please, isn't there anything else we can do? Couldn't we explain to everybody what happened so my reputation wouldn't be ruined? There has to be some way out of this predicament besides marriage to . . . to . . . him!"

"Oh, Sophia," Aunt Nora said, giving an exasperated sigh, "how naïve you are. There is nothing to do now except marry Mr. Huntley. The *ton* would never accept anything less than a marriage now." Aunt Nora pulled Sophia to her feet, gripping both her shoulders and forcing Sophia to look at her. "I think you've embarrassed me enough, don't you, dear? Now, let's go back in and put an end to your shame by getting you properly married."

Sophia looked in Aunt Nora's eyes for several long moments. What she saw was disheartening. Aunt Nora had a hard and challenging look. Sophia realized in that instant that she had never had a friend in Aunt Nora. She almost felt the force of dislike coming through her gaze. Sophia felt completely helpless, and it was an unfamiliar feeling. She nodded. "Yes, of course," she acquiesced. "Let's return to the church."

Aunt Nora smiled a vindictive smile. She had won this little confrontation with ease. Then she turned and led the way back.

As they walked past the row of carriages standing outside the church, Sophia saw something that triggered a memory—a trunk with crisscrossing straps. She stared at it for several moments before realizing that this was Mr. Huntley's trunk; she had counted those very straps to fall asleep in his room. As she stood gawking, two servants carried her trunk and set it on the back of Mr. Huntley's carriage, right next to the trunk with the crisscross straps. Her very own trunk was being tied to the back of Mr. Huntley's carriage.

Her emotions were so wrung out that she should have been past feeling by now, but seeing her trunk on Mr. Huntley's carriage was like a sharp slap of reality. She was about to walk into the church, and when she walked out, she would be leaving in Mr. Huntley's carriage. Just as her trunk was tied to his carriage, she would be tied to him.

"Sophia, come along!" Sophia looked up from where she had stopped on the pavement to stare at the trunk. Aunt Nora was walking into the church. The door slowly closed after her, and Sophia heard Aunt Nora's voice growing fainter as she said, "She's ready now. She'll be right in. Let's get started, shall we?"

Sophia was less ready than ever, but there was nothing else she could do. Mr. Huntley's parting words replayed in her head: *We either get married or your reputation is ruined.*

Slowly, Sophia looked up as the realization dawned. *We either get married or your reputation is ruined.* Mr. Huntley had said there was no choice, but that sounded like a choice to her. She didn't *have* to marry Mr. Huntley! Sophia knew that a ruined reputation meant she couldn't marry anyone, but wasn't no marriage better than an awful one? Could she do it? Could she be a ruined woman? It wasn't an ideal situation, certainly, but it had to be better than marrying that man.

Yes. If her choice was Mr. Huntley or nothing, she chose nothing. She felt a sense of freedom expand in her chest as she seized the thought and began walking quickly. Within a very few steps, she started to run. Slippers and her long gown weren't ideal for running, but Sophia did her best not to let them slow her down. Within moments, she was out of sight of the church. When she first stopped to catch her breath, she looked back and couldn't even see the church spire.

She knew she couldn't go home. There was only one other family she knew in London apart from Aunt Nora, and that was Lord and Lady Fitzgerald.

Eleven

Alex immediately regretted his harsh words, but his anger and frustration had been building up. An accidental ruination would have been bad enough, but once he realized that he had been caught in a well-plotted trap, he had been furious. He was sure that Lady Bloomfield and Miss Spencer had planned the whole thing.

When Lady Bloomfield wouldn't allow him to see Miss Spencer that first day, he wondered what purpose or what new scheme was being carried out. But at the next meeting with both ladies, where Miss Spencer had asked to delay the wedding, he's begun to think that maybe she was innocent. Of course, he couldn't tell for sure; it could have all been an act. But when they arrived at the church and Lady Bloomfield used her patronizing tone to manipulate her niece's emotional state again, he could see that Miss Spencer had not plotted at all. He should have been relieved that at least the woman he was being forced to marry wasn't devious, but somehow his anger had just intensified. Why didn't she stand up to her aunt? Why hadn't she explained her innocence when they were first found together? Or better yet, why didn't she prevent the situation from ever occurring?

With these thoughts rolling through his mind, he'd had no patience for her tentative questions and requests for reassurance.

Oh, but why had he let his vigilant control over his anger slip then? He had been careful to hide his distress in front of Charles and Lucy, who felt endlessly guilty that this had happened at their ball, and he had more than five years of experience of burying the anger he felt toward his father and even Miss Harriet Towler. But he had taken all his frustration out on Miss Spencer, who in merely a few moments would become Mrs. Huntley. With a huge sigh of guilt, he started toward the back of the church. He felt that his anger toward her was partly justified, but he had two sisters' worth of experience to know that it didn't matter. He would have to apologize and give her the encouragement she needed. It truly wasn't *all* her fault, and now that his anger was dispelled, he could see that she must be feeling awful. And he had just made it worse.

Before he reached the door, however, Lady Bloomfield came in saying that Sophia was ready and it was time to begin. Well, they would be married forever; there would be plenty of time to apologize after the ceremony.

He moved back to the front of the church and waited for Miss Spencer to join him. The muffled conversations quieted, and after several long moments, heads began to swivel back toward the door. No one said anything. It was longer than it should have been, and she still hadn't come in. Still, no one spoke.

They all soon looked at Lady Bloomfield for answers, Alex included, thinking she must know why Miss Spencer hadn't come in yet. Lady Bloomfield looked extremely annoyed as she rose from her seat and headed outside to fetch Miss Spencer. Alex decided that Miss Spencer must be hesitating because of the way he had spoken to her, and he felt ashamed of himself. He walked past the few guests on his way out of the church to find Miss Spencer. It looked like the apology would come before the ceremony after all.

Alex couldn't see Lady Bloomfield or Miss Spencer when he stepped outside, so he retraced the walk that they had taken before he had stormed back into the building. As he came around the corner of the church, he could hear Lady Bloomfield as she rushed around the headstones calling in an angry whisper, "Sophia, come out this instant! You are embarrassing me! Is this any way to repay my kindness to you?" Alex felt a twinge of apprehension. Where had she gone? It was as though she had vanished into the air.

Soon Charles and Lucy came out too, and then several other guests. They all looked for Miss Spencer, Lady Bloomfield the most frantic among them, but she was nowhere to be found.

Finally, Alex asked the coachmen if any they had seen Miss Spencer, and one of them said he didn't know who Miss Spencer was, but he had seen a young lady run by a few minutes back. He pointed in the direction she had gone.

Now Alex was worried. She shouldn't be alone in London, especially on foot. He looked around, caught Charles's attention, and beckoned him over. "Charles, Miss Spencer seems to have run away in that general direction," he said, gesturing with his hand. "Will you and Lucy look on several of the streets to the south? I'll take the north. Let's meet back at your house once we find her."

He hardly waited for Charles's reply before he headed toward his carriage. Before climbing in, Alex turned to Lady Bloomfield, who was about to climb into her own carriage. She was seething with indignation.

"I don't know who is more to blame, Lady Bloomfield," Alex said, "you or me, but we can't right the wrongs until she is found. I think it would be best if you return to your home in case she turns up there. If she does arrive, please send a note to the Evertons." Lady Bloomfield looked at him in furious disbelief, but he didn't wait for a reply. He just climbed up next to the coachman and drove off in the direction that Miss Spencer had fled.

Twelve

*L*uckily, Sophia remembered that the Fitzgeralds' London resi-dence was called Dalton House, and that it was on the north-west side. That was enough information for the driver of the coach she hailed to get her there. Although the coach carried her to her destination, she felt the excitement from her daring escape was carrying her.

Up until a few days ago, Sophia had thought that Sir Henry and Lady Anne Fitzgerald were still at the seaside. They had gone months and months ago at her father's recommendation. Little William had had a rough case of bronchitis last winter, and her father thought the sea air would speed his recovery. But one eve-ning last week, when she and Aunt Nora went to Haymarket The-atre, Sophia had spotted Lady Anne from a distance.

Sophia was already tired by that point. She remembered fol-lowing closely behind Aunt Nora as they made their way to their box. A large crowd was there that night, and Aunt Nora had moved brusquely through it. Sophia followed as closely as she could but kept being jostled as she tried to keep up. She was tempted to reach forward, take hold of Aunt Nora's purple gown, and let her tow her along, but even Sophia knew that wouldn't be proper.

They finally reached their box only to find it was just as crowded as the passageways had been. After squeezing their way to the side corner where their reserved seats were, Sophia slumped down in her chair to wait for the performance to begin.

With her eyes staring vacantly at the opposite side of the room, her sleepy mind recognized Lady Anne. Sophia immediately perked up and waved to get Lady Anne's attention, but without success. She watched as Sir Henry entered the box and sat beside his wife, and she continued waving to get their attention. Aunt Nora noticed her gestures. "Sophia, what are you doing?" she asked.

"I know them!" she replied excitedly. "That's Sir Henry and Lady Anne Fitzgerald. They live at Tissington Park."

Aunt Nora quickly put her hand on Sophia's arm. "Don't make a spectacle, please." Then glancing at the stage, she said, "The performance is beginning. You will have to wait to say hello to your friends."

Sophia was distracted throughout the performance by Sir Henry and Lady Anne's presence. She continuously glanced their way to make sure they were still there and to see if they happened to look her way, but they never did.

She was also unable to make her way through the crush of people to reach them after the play ended. It was far too crowded, and Aunt Nora was anxious to leave. Once they were in the carriage, Sophia said, "I can't believe we were so close and they didn't notice me. But now that I know they're in town, Aunt Nora, may we pay a visit to Lady Anne tomorrow?"

Aunt Nora looked disbelievingly at Sophia. "You're not serious, of course? You know that it would be very improper."

Sophia wasn't able to think of a reason why it would be improper, but not wanting Aunt Nora to realize her ignorance, she merely asked, "Surely with such old acquaintances, it wouldn't be too unseemly?"

Aunt Nora must have realized that Sophia didn't quite understand. "Lord and Lady Fitzgerald are quite a step above you in society," she patronizingly explained. "You will have to wait until you receive some formal recognition from the Fitzgeralds before you can claim the acquaintance."

Sophia hadn't realized that the rules of high society would be enforced on an acquaintance from home. At the time, she was grateful for her aunt's greater knowledge on such matters, thinking that she really wasn't a close friend of the Fitzgeralds. She had been to Tissington Park several times with her father when he was sent for, and Lady Anne invited all the young ladies of the village to tea once a year. And occasionally the Fitzgeralds hosted a picnic. But after feeling so lost in the crowds of London, seeing Lady Anne's familiar face had felt like seeing her dearest friend again.

Sophia looked for Lady Anne and Sir Henry at every event she'd attended with Aunt Nora after that, but she hadn't seen them again.

As the carriage pulled to a stop in front of their door, Sophia stepped down from it and paid the driver. Her heart beat wildly. Were the Fitzgeralds still in London? Would they be offended by her arrival at their doorstep asking for help? Aunt Nora had said it would be improper to force them into acknowledging her in town, but all she could do was hope that the Fitzgeralds would overlook the impertinence because of her desperate situation.

◦~◦

Lady Anne Fitzgerald had just finished dressing and was trying to decide if she should spend the morning with her children in the nursery or pay a visit to Lady Jennings, who always knew the latest gossip. Before she could make up her mind, Harold, her butler, appeared at the door of her sitting room. "There is a young lady here to see you, Lady Anne," he said. "Her name is Miss Spencer."

Lady Anne searched her thoughts for a moment, trying to place the familiar name. The only person she could think of was Sophia Spencer, the doctor's lovely daughter back in Tissington. Lady Anne was sure that couldn't be who was waiting for her below. She gave Harold a skeptical smile. "Are you sure that's the young lady's name?" She rose as she spoke. She was curious who her caller really was and moved toward the door.

"She didn't present a card or say where she came from," Harold responded, "but the name she gave me is Sophia Spencer."

Lady Anne paused as she registered the unexpected news. How could Sophia Spencer possibly be in London? She moved with avid curiosity to find out why Sophia Spencer was calling on her in London of all places.

She descended the stairs and was quite surprised that indeed it was Mr. Spencer's daughter waiting in her entry hall. "Sophia Spencer! When Harold told me who my visitor was, I was quite sure it was a mistake. How did you come to be in London? It's just so unexpected to see someone from Tissington here in town." Lady Anne took Sophia by arm. She seemed tense, and Lady Anne was instantly worried about what might be distressing her, but despite her anxious state, she came willingly with Lady Anne to the drawing room. "Did you have a nice journey? I hope there is nothing wrong at home. Your father is well?"

Sophia nodded and then found her voice. "Yes, Father is well, but I didn't arrive from Tissington. I've been in London several weeks." Lady Anne was surprised at this news too, but she let Sophia continue. "I've been staying with my aunt, Lady Bloomfield, but I was supposed to be married today, and I didn't want to, so I ran away." Sophia's voice cracked at the end of her words as she struggled not to cry. But when Lady Anne wrapped her arms around the poor girl, Sophia couldn't fight it any longer and dissolved into tears.

Lady Anne was quite shocked. She had heard the gossip that Lady Bloomfield's niece had been caught with a gentleman at the Evertons' ball and a wedding was imminent to cover up the whole affair. But she had no idea that Sophia was Lady Bloomfield's niece.

Lady Anne hadn't paid close attention to the details of the scandal before because she didn't know those involved that well. But now she was determined to know everything. "Sophia, dear, are you saying the wedding was this morning?"

Sophia couldn't manage words yet, but she nodded in confirmation.

"And you left before the wedding could take place? So you are not yet married?"

Again Sophia nodded miserably, but Lady Anne wasn't sure which question she was answering. "You *are* married?"

Sophia shook her head no. After a few sniffs, she was able to speak again. "I spoke to Mr. Huntley before the wedding, but he was so angry with me that I knew I just couldn't marry him. So I ran away." Sophia's tone became defensive as she added, "I know it means my reputation will stay ruined, but I don't care."

Lady Anne kept her thoughts to herself on that point and instead asked Sophia to tell her everything that had happened, starting from the beginning.

Sophia told Lady Anne about arriving in London several weeks back, and that her aunt was chaperoning her through the Season. Then she described how everything had quickly fallen apart when she fell asleep at a ball. Sophia emphasized the unfairness of it all, and Lady Anne completely sympathized with her on that point.

Lady Anne had known Sophia Spencer for years. When the young ladies from the village came to Tissington Park for tea, Sophia was always her favorite. Mr. Spencer had taken great care to teach his daughter to be a lady and, although it had been a financial hardship for them, he had engaged a governess to ensure a superior education. But that wasn't her only advantage. She seemed to be the leader of the group of girls her age, a role that she filled without condescension. Whenever an argument arose or an unkind word was said, Sophia would diffuse the situation with ease. And she wasn't just a cheerful girl; she seemed to be genuinely happy.

It was such a shame to see her distressed to the point of tears. Sophia had risen to the top of society in their small village with no effort. London was different, however. With artifice and hidden rules, it was difficult to navigate London Society, and Sophia obviously hadn't been able to do it.

Lady Anne knew who Lady Nora Bloomfield was by sight, and with Lord and Lady Everton it was the same. They mixed in slightly different circles. But she had never heard of Mr. Huntley. How she would help Sophia out of this mess, she didn't know. But Sophia Spencer didn't deserve a forced marriage or a ruined reputation.

After concluding her story, Sophia said, "I just want to go home, Lady Anne. Do you think you will be returning to Tissington soon? Or could you help me hire a coach and a maid so I could return home?"

Lady Anne instantly realized that Sophia didn't understand the consequences of what she was suggesting. In London, a ruined reputation would make any young lady a social exile, but in Tissington, it would be worse. All of Sophia's friends would turn on her as soon as they heard about her London adventures. "Ahhh . . . I'm sure your father would want you to stay with us until we can bring you home."

Lady Anne could see Sophia's hesitation to agree with such a plan. The longing for home would be natural at such a moment as this, but Lady Anne knew that returning to Tissington wouldn't solve anything.

"When will you be going home, exactly?" Sophia tentatively asked.

An idea began to form in Lady Anne's mind and she wrapped her arm around Sophia once more. "Sir Henry is attending Parliament, and it will be over in a few weeks. After that, we can all journey back to Tissington together. Until then, consider yourself our guest."

Sophia's desire to return to Tissington right away was evident—she tried another excuse. "I'd hate to put you to so much trouble, having me as a guest."

But Lady Anne was all reassurance as she rang the bell for the servant. In between ordering a room to be made ready for Miss Spencer and tea to be served, Lady Anne continued to comfort Sophia. "Not to worry, dear. You've obviously been put through more than anyone could be expected to cope with. Let me take care of you now, and I'm sure everything will come out right."

These words of sympathy produced a watery smile from Sophia.

Sophia was about to leave the room to follow a servant to a guest chamber when she suddenly turned back and exclaimed, "I forgot! I don't have my things. My trunk is . . . er . . ." Lady Anne waited expectantly until Sophia finally admitted, "Mr. Huntley has it. I had better send a note asking to have it sent here. And perhaps I should send a note to Aunt Nora, so she knows where I am. But I don't care what she says! I'm not returning home with her." Sophia was defiant as she said this, and Lady Anne didn't try to persuade her otherwise. She rather hoped to keep Sophia with her until she could resolve the whole issue.

Sophia was shown to the desk and wrote the notes, and Lady Anne had them sent directly. Lady Anne also encouraged Sophia to write a longer letter to her father relating the change in her circumstances. While Sophia wrote, Lady Anne directed the servants to prepare a room for Sophia so she could rest. She also directed that tea be brought. Knowing that she would likely soon have visitors looking for Miss Sophia Spencer, Lady Anne encouraged Sophia to lie down for a while. And Sophia, who looked incredibly tired after her ordeal, readily complied.

Thirteen

Alex returned to the Evertons' after a fruitless search. He prayed that Miss Spencer was somewhere safe by this point; it had been more than two hours. Upon entering, he met Lucy. Her expectant face matched his, and they both quickly realized that the other had no news. With sympathy, Lucy said, "Charles is still out searching for Miss Spencer, but I came back to the house to see if you returned."

"Thank you, Lucy." The words were inadequate. He should have said more, but he was too worried about Miss Spencer. He was lamenting as much to himself as to Lucy when he said, "This is my fault. If anything happens to her, the blame is mine."

"Alex, I'm sure we'll find her soon, but you can't take responsibility for her actions."

"No, it's my actions I'm responsible for. When we spoke outside the church, I lost my temper with her," he admitted.

Lucy gave him a sympathetic look but didn't respond, and

Alex felt all over again how wrong he had been. Standing around talking about it would never fix things, so he turned toward the door and said, "I'd better keep looking."

"Wait, Alex. I know you feel terrible, but have something to eat before you go out again."

Before she could continue to persuade him, a servant arrived with a note addressed to Mr. A. Huntley. Quickly scanning to the bottom, he saw that the note was signed by Miss Spencer. He breathed a sigh of relief as he quickly read through its contents.

> *Mr. Huntley,*
>
> You said we had to get married or my reputation was ruined. I have decided to accept the consequences of a ruined reputation. I'm sure you will be as pleased as I am to put this incident behind us. I will be leaving London as soon as it can be arranged. Would you please have my trunk delivered to Lord Fitzgerald at Dalton House?
>
> I am terribly sorry that you were forced to go to so much trouble on my behalf. It really was an innocent mistake. Thank you for being willing to save my reputation, even though you so obviously didn't want to.
>
> Cordially,
>
> *Miss S. Spencer*

Alex finished reading the note with very mixed feelings. Foremost was relief that not only was Miss Spencer safe, but also that he knew exactly where to find her. But that feeling was closely followed by exasperation that she thought the marriage didn't have to take place. Was she really so naïve to think that the events of the past few days could be waved away with a simple note? The marriage was inevitable. Not only was her reputation at stake but his honor depended on it as well. She said she would accept the consequences, but she couldn't realize what those would be, or she would not so readily make such a choice. Miss Spencer thought she was making things easier on him, but really Alex's troubles had just multiplied.

His shame also intensified as he reread the end of the note: the part about him so obviously not wanting to marry her. Alex gave a resigned sigh as he thought of the task ahead of him. *The very marriage I didn't want I now have to go and beg for,* he thought. His pride balked at the idea, but he knew he had brought this on himself. And after the way he had treated her, convincing Miss Sophia Spencer to marry him would not be an easy task.

"Well, she's safe at Dalton House with Lord and Lady Fitzgerald," Alex informed Lucy. She immediately began to ask questions about why and how and so on. Of course, Alex didn't have any of those answers. He asked Lucy to pass on the information they had to the others who were looking for her as he headed out to his carriage once again.

As he drove, he cursed himself once more for losing his temper. Up to that point, he had felt himself to be the innocent target of a plot, but now his problems were compounded, and he had only himself to blame.

Alex arrived at Dalton House and was received by Lady Fitzgerald. In an imposing manner she asked him, "So, you are Mr. Huntley?" After Alex's terse nod, she went on. "I am Lady Anne Fitzgerald. You may call me Lady Anne." It wasn't so much a request as a command.

Alex had little patience for introductions. He needed to speak to Miss Spencer and talk her into marrying him. Not seeing her in the room caused the first stirrings of alarm. "Lady Anne, is Miss Spencer here? She hasn't left, has she?" he asked.

"Yes, she's here, Mr. Huntley," Lady Anne was quick to reply. "I will send for her in a few minutes. I wanted to have a word with you before she comes down."

Alex's first thought was that he had another conniving woman to deal with. *What terms will be forced upon me this time?* he thought. After dealing with Miss Spencer's aunt, he wasn't sure how much more of this he could take. But before he could deliver a rude retort, Lady Anne continued, "Sophia explained to me what has happened, but I can't make sense of any of it. It seems very much from the way she spoke, that her aunt, Lady Bloomfield, must be the one to blame for everything. Sophia never said so, and actually, I don't think it even occurred to her. She thinks it was all an innocent mistake, but I cannot agree. I know Lady Bloomfield only a little, and I can't think of a reason why she would want to force her niece into a marriage with you."

Alex's initial impression of Lady Anne quickly gave way to a better one in a matter of a few minutes. If she suspected Lady Bloomfield without even speaking with her, then she must be very astute. "I can't find any motivation either, Lady Anne. I am not wealthy; in fact, I am trying to escape from debt. I never expected to be the mark of such a plot as this. The only conclusion I have come to is that she wants to make us miserable. Perhaps she is just trying to rid herself of Miss Spencer, but if so, why would she have invited her for the Season?"

"Why indeed?" Lady Anne mused. There was obviously a missing piece, and Lady Anne appeared to be thinking hard as to what it might be. But besides Lady Bloomfield's motivation, they had other things to discuss.

"Mr. Huntley," Lady Anne went on, "Sophia has asked that we help her return home to her father. It would be no problem for us to hire a carriage and send her home today, but I think I've convinced her to stay in London with us for the next few weeks and return to Tissington in our carriage."

Distressed by this news, Alex exclaimed, "But we were supposed to be married today! I was hoping to convince her to return to St. Luke's tomorrow and marry me. It has to be done." Alex's ears turned a bit pink. "We were caught in what was a very . . . compromising situation. I know she thinks that a ruined reputation is something she can handle, but you must see that she can't simply remain in London with you."

Lady Anne seemed almost pleased with Alex's view of the situation. Apparently, she thought of it in the same light that he did. She had a gleam in her eye, and he once more wondered if she wasn't scheming somehow. With complete confidence, she responded, "Mr. Huntley, you are quite right. The only way Sophia can remain in London is for her to marry you, *or* if she is *planning* to marry you." She paused to let him think on that for a moment. "We can tell everyone that you are engaged, and that the wedding has just been postponed for a few weeks so you can be married in Tissington."

Alex shook his head. "That really won't solve any—"

"At this point," Lady Anne interrupted, "all Sophia wants is to run away and put this all behind her. But you and I know that can't happen. It would take a miracle to convince her that marriage is better than a ruined reputation right now. What we need is time for you to court her. We'll tell her that it's a fake engagement, just so she can remain in London until we can take her home. And hopefully, well before the time is up, you can convince her to make it a real engagement."

Alex didn't like this plan any better than his own. In fact, he felt it was worse. Now he'd have to court Miss Spencer in town for the next few weeks when he should have been home three days ago. His new steward would have to manage things without him a while longer, though, because the only thing more important than recovering his family estate was recovering his honor. "I think you are right, Lady Anne." She expelled her held breath and then gave Alex an open and friendly smile.

"Those are my favorite words to hear, Mr. Huntley."

He answered her with a little smile and a slight shake of his head. He truly hoped her plan would work.

Lady Anne had one more thing to say. "I should tell you that I think very highly of Miss Spencer. Her father is a country doctor, but he has made many sacrifices to bring her up as a lady. Besides her fine manners and education, she has something else . . . something that I'm not even sure how to describe." Lady Anne paused, her face scrunched up in thought. "It's that . . . she tries so hard to improve herself." Lady Anne shrugged, acknowledging that her description was inadequate. "I think, Mr. Huntley, that you will have to get to know Sophia for yourself."

Alex listened quite intently to Lady Anne's description of Sophia, and for the first time since the Evertons' ball, the thought crossed his mind that marrying her might not be the worst thing imaginable. This was the first positive word he had heard spoken about Miss Spencer; her aunt had been far less complimentary. Marrying her still wasn't his choice, but maybe they would eventually get along after all.

Fourteen

Sophia awoke from her nap with a gentle rap on her door. She was confused to be waking up in a strange room with the sun shining in. She called out, "Just a moment!" as she tried to remember where she was. The voice at the door unraveled the mystery for her. "Miss Spencer, Lady Fitzgerald sent to ask if you would like an audience with Mr. Huntley, who is here to call on you."

As the events of the day rushed back to her, Sophia immediately straightened her gown and smoothed her hair. She was beginning to hate waking up to face unpleasant things.

"Yes . . . ah, yes," she called through the door. "Please tell them I'll be down in just a few moments." But her voice wasn't quite steady as she said it. She wasn't sure what to expect from Mr. Huntley. She had hoped that he would be so grateful at not having to marry her that he would just send her trunk with a servant. Their last conversation had been awful. As she walked down to the drawing room, she felt her stomach drop with dreadful anticipation.

All she had thought about Mr. Huntley since she ran away from the church that morning was how relieved he must be that she was choosing a ruined reputation over him. But now that he was here and wanted to speak to her, she realized that his reaction might be angry rather than grateful. He might not have wanted that wedding, but he likely didn't want to be left standing at the altar either. Once again, she felt like kicking herself for acting selfishly. She still wouldn't have gone through with the ceremony, but maybe she could have told Mr. Huntley that she was leaving.

Well, if he was going to shout at her again, this time she would show him how much "backbone" she had. Sophia lifted her head, took a deep breath, and entered the drawing room, feeling prepared to withstand anything.

Mr. Huntley bowed and Lady Anne smiled as she came in, and then an awkward silence ensued. Sophia noticed a look of encouragement pass from Lady Anne to Mr. Huntley, which seemed to spur him to speak.

"Miss Spencer, I need to apologize for the way I spoke to you earlier today." He paused, cringing as if in remembrance of what he had said. "I was feeling such a victim of the circumstances and I took it out on you, and I'm sorry." She watched him trace his finger along the back of the chair he was standing beside, probably so he wouldn't have to meet Sophia's gaze. When Sophia didn't reply, he finished with, "I really do feel terrible for the things I said."

Sophia hadn't replied because she was feeling a bit unsettled. She had come in the room prepared to defend herself against an irate lecture and instead had received a heartfelt apology. She stumbled over her words a bit as she tried to articulate her reply. "It's fine . . . erm, you must have . . . or, rather, I was feeling just the same way. A victim, I mean."

"Of course," Mr. Huntley replied, lifting his gaze to meet Sophia's for a moment.

After another silence, although a slightly less awkward one this time, Sophia sat down, allowing Mr. Huntley to do the same.

"Sophia, since you will be staying here for the next few weeks," Lady Anne said, "I've asked Mr. Huntley a favor. Obviously your reputation has been compromised, so you won't be able to set foot out the door unless it's widely known that a wedding is expected between you two. And Mr. Huntley has agreed to this plan."

Sophia's jaw dropped in dismay. "Do you mean everyone will think we still plan to marry?"

She saw Lady Anne exchange a silent look with Mr. Huntley before answering. "It's really the only way for you to remain in London with me until we return to Tissington."

Sophia was about to protest this plan, but Lady Anne began speaking in a persuasive tone. "I'm sure I couldn't enjoy your visit at all if I knew you were practically a prisoner in my home. Sir Henry will feel just as I do, I'm sure. For us to really enjoy having you as our guest, we'll need to visit our friends and introduce you to them. If you and Mr. Huntley profess that you plan to marry, then it won't be a problem at all. However, if you feel you don't like my plan, then I suppose you and I will have to remain inside for the duration of your visit."

"Lady Anne, I would hate to put you through any of that. It all sounds terribly inconvenient. If you could just assist me, I'd much rather hire a carriage and return home," Sophia quickly suggested.

Lady Anne thought a moment. "Sophia, there's no need for all that expense and trouble when we have plenty of room for you in our carriage." She sounded genuinely caring. "And besides, I *want* you to stay. Sir Henry is so busy in the House of Lords that I feel quite lonely here in town. It would be so kind of you to stay and keep me company."

Sophia still hesitated. "But does it not seem dishonest? I would feel so guilty telling everyone we intend to marry when we don't."

"Sophia, one little fib should be the least of your worries. Why, you have been honest all along in proclaiming your innocence about what happened at the ball. But as you told me yourself, no one believed the truth. Besides, you'll only be deceiving London society, and as they are the ones who have forced you into this predicament, surely there is no reason to feel guilty."

Sophia could see the logic in that. In fact, the whole plan made sense. The only argument she had left was that she didn't want to. But hadn't she just resolved—again—to think of others before herself? Sophia had a very high regard for Lady Anne, and while she didn't want to pretend an engagement, she did want to please Lady Anne.

And the most persuasive point in favor of Lady Anne's plan was that Mr. Huntley seemed happy to go along with it. If he had been angry with her, as she had fully expected him to be, then she wouldn't have agreed to be in his company no matter what.

"Your plan is probably the best, Lady Anne." Her eyes shifted to Mr. Huntley, and she saw that he looked pleased, almost smiling, in fact. Turning back to Lady Anne, she said, "At first I thought it was just postponing the inevitable, but I see that we can have a lovely few weeks together if Mr. Huntley and I appear to be engaged."

"Perfect," exclaimed Lady Anne. "Now I won't have to cancel anything. On Thursday there is a musical trio performing at the Ashbys', and I'm sure Lady Ashby would hold it against me if I were to cancel this late. Instead, I'll send a note that there will be two more in our party. I really am so pleased."

It seemed as if all was now arranged, and Sophia expected Mr. Huntley to take his leave any moment. But he stayed in the room, discussing several trivial things with Lady Anne before asking, "Lady Anne, may I have a private word with Miss Spencer?"

Lady Anne looked as though she couldn't leave the room fast enough. She quickly agreed and was out the door before Sophia could quiet the feeling of dread that had come with Mr. Huntley's request. Why did he want a private word? During the only other private conversation they'd had, he'd been quite angry. Maybe he hadn't meant that apology at all, and perhaps he was still angry or even angrier and was waiting until they had no audience to tell her what he really thought of this mess she had gotten them both into.

She took a deep breath before looking up at Mr. Huntley. That was when she was finally able to calm her nervousness. Every time she had spoken with him he had seemed so composed, never showing much emotion at all—except right before the wedding, of course. But looking at him now she could see he was nervous as well. He could hardly look at her as he spoke.

"I just wanted to say . . . the first thing . . . well, I need to tell you again how sorry I am for the way I spoke to you today. I haven't lost my temper like that in years, and I am so sorry that I took my anger out on you."

His hesitant manner helped Sophia feel more confident with each passing moment. And that confidence allowed her to say what she knew she should.

"I understand, and I hope you will accept my apology as well. I'm so sorry for falling asleep in your room and for not putting a stop to the wedding much sooner. And . . . I shouldn't have left you at the church without at least telling you that you didn't have to marry me. I'm sorry I just . . . ran off," she finished flatly.

"Yes, you shouldn't have run off. I was worried about what might've happened to you alone on the streets of London," said Mr. Huntley.

Sophia was surprised; she hadn't worried once about her safety. She had felt as though she was running away from danger and into refuge as she lost herself in the crowd that morning.

"As for the rest," Mr. Huntley went on, "I don't think you have anything to be sorry for. You are quite blameless in all this, aren't you?" It was hardly a question; Mr. Huntley stated it as if he was sure.

Without waiting for her to argue the point, Mr. Huntley changed the subject. "The other thing I wanted to discuss . . . or rather ask you, Miss Spencer, is if you will go for a drive in the park with me tomorrow."

Her brow wrinkled with worry. "Oh, I suppose we must be seen out together for Lady Anne's plan to work. Er . . . yes then, I suppose a drive in the park is as good a way as any." Sophia wasn't enthusiastic about the plan, but she also realized that it was all being done for her and that Lord and Lady Fitzgerald and Mr. Huntley were doing all this to help her in this strange circumstance.

"I'll pick you up in the carriage tomorrow morning, then. That is, unless . . . I'm sorry . . . I should have asked before: do you ride?"

"Yes. Yes, I do." Sophia felt a small glimmer of enthusiasm grow inside her. "I love to ride, and I haven't had a chance since I've been in London."

"Then as long as the weather stays nice, we'll ride instead," Mr. Huntley replied, and for the first time since she met Mr. Huntley, Sophia smiled.

When Alex saw Sophia smile, he realized that she was pretty. Up to this point, he'd thought she was an exact copy of every other young lady in London for the Season. No distinguishing features had stood out. When he met with her before the wedding, he admitted to himself that she wasn't plain, but he certainly hadn't been in the frame of mind to find any beauty in her. Now, however, she smiled at him as though she saw him as an ally, even if it was just temporarily. That one friendly smile was contagious, and he returned it naturally. He'd never believed that such a gesture could be exchanged between them. He nodded his head and lost himself in the thought for a moment before recollecting himself and taking his leave.

Two of the Fitzgeralds' servants attended him to the carriage to retrieve Miss Spencer's trunk, and he drove back to the Evertons to have his own trunk unloaded again. For the rest of the day, Alex thought about Miss Spencer. The wedding was delayed but still inevitable, and he was beginning to think about her character and how they would suit each other. He had watched Miss Spencer throughout her exchange with Lady Anne. He had seen in action how emotions crossed her features. First dismay—because she so obviously didn't like the arrangement—but then chagrin because she obviously regretted her inward thoughts. Determination next, followed immediately by eagerness to please Lady Anne. It was fascinating to watch.

Interesting too was Lady Anne's ability to manage her young friend. She had the same talent for persuasion that Lady Bloomfield seemed to possess, only she used her talent for good.

Miss Spencer had a complete lack of suspicion that she was being manipulated. She seemed too innocent, and Alex recalled how he had trusted others so completely once and had been severely let down. It had led to years of hard work and recovery for him, as well as an untrusting nature. He hoped that Miss Spencer would come through this experience without completely losing her faith in others.

Fifteen

Sophia watched from the window as Mr. Huntley's carriage rolled out of sight. She breathed a sigh of resignation. It would not be easy to pretend to be engaged. He had apologized beautifully, and she said she forgave him, but she hadn't really. He had been so mean and unfair . . . she wouldn't forget it anytime soon. But he was helping her now by staying in London to pretend to be engaged. She wondered why and concluded that if he were truly sorry, then it must be out of guilt. Perhaps he *did* deserve her forgiveness. She sighed again; she'd have to work on that. There would be plenty of opportunities to do so while she was pretending to be engaged to him.

Still gazing out the window, Sophia suddenly spotted something familiar—Aunt Nora's carriage. She quickly backed away from the window. She was dreading this encounter; it was sure to be unpleasant. Sophia knew it was cowardly, but she ran out of the room to find Lady Anne so that she wouldn't have to face her aunt's ire alone. As a result, Aunt Nora was shown into the drawing room and was waiting for them when Sophia followed Lady Anne into the room.

Aunt Nora greeted Lady Anne, but her gaze kept flicking to Sophia impatiently. Lady Anne invited her to sit and began pouring tea. While she did so, Aunt Nora turned her attention on Sophia and smiled rigidly. "Do you realize how worried we've all been, Sophia?" The reprimand in her words was almost unnoticeable because her voice was honey sweet, almost loving. "You frightened me so by disappearing the way you did."

Sophia didn't answer right away. The last time she spoke with Aunt Nora, her aunt's words and voice had been harsh. She had looked at Sophia with such severity that it felt like hatred. And now she was sitting in the Fitzgeralds' drawing room, acting quite the opposite. This duplicity was something Sophia had never experienced. She knew that people who loved you were loving, like her father. People who were indifferent to you ignored you, like most of the older generation in her village. And people who despised you were unkind, like Martha Bullock from Tissington. Her experiences up to now didn't include this kind of deception that Aunt Nora seemed so skilled at.

Sophia crossed her arms in front of herself defensively. "I didn't realize how worried you would be, Aunt Nora," Sophia said, wanting to sound confident but coming across as petulant.

Aunt Nora's smile grew tighter, as if she were grinding her teeth together. But she seemed to hide the tension when she spoke. "Of course I was worried. How could you think otherwise? Thank goodness you sent a note so I was able to find you. There should be enough time, though. We need to leave to get you to St. Luke's before the vicar leaves for the day."

Sophia knew she didn't have to do as Aunt Nora said, but that didn't stop their feeling of panic. "I'm staying here with the Fitzgeralds," Sophia declared, scooting closer to Lady Anne.

Aunt Nora noticed the movement. "Of course Lady Fitzgerald should come too," she said. "I'm sorry I didn't realize how close you were to her, or she would have been invited to the wedding in the first place."

With a residual desire to not upset her aunt, Sophia's voice wavered as she responded. "No, what I meant to say was I'm not . . . I'm not getting married."

Aunt Nora's smile stayed pasted on her face, but her eyes turned fiery and her nostrils flared, the combination making her look strange and fierce. Sophia leaned even farther away in fear. She was left with no doubt that Aunt Nora truly despised her.

Aunt Nora quickly masked her emotions, but before she could use a falsely gentle voice to lecture Sophia on saving her reputation by marriage, Lady Anne spoke. "What Miss Spencer means to say is she isn't getting married at St. Luke's. She and Mr. Huntley will be married at the Tissington Parish when we escort them there in a few weeks' time." She said it with such certainty that even though Sophia knew it was a lie, it still increased her feeling of unease.

Aunt Nora's gaze flicked between Lady Anne and Sophia. Aunt Nora couldn't hide her annoyance, but she also seemed less inclined to argue the point now. "They will be married then?" she asked for clarification.

Lady Anne, who had finished pouring the tea, merely inclined her head as a response. Aunt Nora accepted the cup that Lady Anne handed her. She seemed satisfied with the news.

"You are unwise to wait," she said to Sophia, "even these few weeks. The only reason I rushed you to St. Luke's was so that you wouldn't suffer."

Sophia didn't respond. She knew that wasn't the only reason. Aunt Nora cared far more about her own reputation than about Sophia's. Sophia was convinced that her aunt wanted her to quickly marry so that she wouldn't suffer by association.

In confirmation of what Sophia was thinking, Aunt Nora said, "I hope you won't regret keeping her with you, Lady Fitzgerald. With this matter unresolved, it might reflect poorly on you."

"It's so kind of you to be concerned, Lady Bloomfield," Lady Anne replied with a smile just as false as Aunt Nora's, "but I'm not worried about that in the least. Sophia has always been a favorite of mine, and Lord Fitzgerald and I are honored to have her as our guest."

Sophia felt her confidence returning with these kind words, and she looked her aunt in the eye when she rose to leave a few minutes later.

Aunt Nora smiled again, but it didn't reach her eyes. "Are you sure you wish to remain here, Sophia? After all, I am family. Perhaps you should return with me until it's time for the Fitzgeralds to escort you home."

Sophia was quite sure that Aunt Nora didn't mean what she said and had no trouble replying, "No, thank you." She justified her refusal by adding, "My trunk has already been delivered here. I think it would be easiest to stay." It was a feeble excuse, but Aunt Nora grasped onto it as though it were valid. She bid them farewell and departed alone.

Sixteen

The next morning, Alex brought Lucy's horse all ready with a sidesaddle for Miss Spencer. As he neared Dalton House, he saw Miss Spencer watching him from an upstairs window. She waved a greeting before turning away. A few moments later, she emerged from the house completely ready to go. Alex was taken aback. The fashion must have changed since the last time he had been part of the London set—and changed for the better. Five years ago, every young lady of his acquaintance would have made him wait at least twenty minutes before any outing, and then she would have looked bored, as if nothing could spark her interest. He had been dreading the outing this morning, but Miss Spencer's enthusiasm was contagious, and Alex was pleased they were going. It was as good a start as he could have hoped for.

Alex chose their direction, and they went directly to Hyde Park. Once they were seen riding there together, an announcement of their continued engagement would be a mere formality.

At first their ride was quiet, which Alex knew wouldn't help him win her over. With only a few weeks in which to court her, he needed to use his time wisely. But knowing that he was supposed to court her made him formal. "Miss Spencer, we've gone through this whole ordeal together," he said rather stiffly, "and yet I feel that I know very little about you. Perhaps you could tell me about Tissington and your life there."

Miss Spencer gave a slight shrug. "I'm sure you won't find it very interesting. Tissington is a fairly small village, and not much goes on there. Tissington Park is Lord and Lady Fitzgerald's country estate, and it's the most noteworthy thing about the town." Miss Spencer turned in her seat and squinted into the sun. They urged their horses forward and she continued, "I've always lived in Tissington with my father. Well, my mother too, but she and a baby sister both died in childbirth when I was just two. Ever since then, it's just been my father and me."

Alex waited for more, but this seemed to be the end of her description. As they rode in silence for several minutes, Alex noted the looks they were receiving. Their progress through the park was being noticed by everyone out enjoying the sunshine.

Directing his attention back to Miss Spencer, Alex tried to get the conversation started again. "Well then, Miss Spencer, what do you enjoy in your spare time?" It sounded scripted to Alex's ears, and he wished for Charles's easy ability with people.

Miss Spencer didn't seem to notice his stiffness. "Well, this, actually," she said, lifting the reins to gesture what she meant. "Riding is my favorite thing to do in my spare time. Although I like a little more variation in my rides than Hyde Park can provide. We have some hills to the south and east of our cottage where I love to go riding." Then, as though she regretted sharing something personal, she added in a more distant tone, "The views are really quite beautiful."

Their formal exchange continued until Miss Spencer took an

opportunity during one of the many awkward pauses to ask, "Mr. Huntley, why did you agree to stay an extra fortnight in town to pretend an engagement with me?"

Alex thought of several answers but settled on the most honest one. "The primary reason was because my honor was at stake."

"Truly? I thought *my* honor was what everyone was worrying so much about."

Alex had to be careful with his response. After a slight hesitation, he replied, "Regardless of whether we are engaged or not, I still feel as though your honor is under my protection. And my honor depends on protecting yours."

Miss Spencer looked at him then, and as she met his eyes, she blushed. "I hate that I've put you in this position." She was about to say more, but at that moment she caught sight of a carriage a little distance away, and a look of recognition crossed her features. "Excuse me a moment, Mr. Huntley. I just want to say hello to some friends. I'll be right back."

⚬⚭⚬

Sophia rode her horse over to the Brights' carriage. She had enjoyed the company of these two young ladies at several events she had attended with Aunt Nora and was happy to see them again. "Hello, Louise! Hello, Lydia!" she said with a friendly smile. "What are you two doing tucked in your carriage? You should be out riding on a beautiful day like this."

The two girls gave each other an almost comically surprised look, but neither of them spoke to Sophia. They looked uncomfortably at their mother, who, looking angry and flustered, leaned forward and called to the coachman, "We won't be stopping here. Drive on."

Sophia couldn't believe what was happening. They weren't even going to acknowledge her! She had never felt so offended and so wronged. But before the coachman could do anything, Mr. Huntley was at Sophia's side motioning for the coachman to wait a moment. "Sophia, won't you introduce me to your friends?" he asked.

Sophia's face was slightly pink from anger and embarrassment, but she quickly caught on. By using her Christian name, Mr. Huntley was playing his role as fiancé in order to save her from this humiliation. So she smoothed her features and in her most formal way said, "Of course. This is Mrs. Bright, Miss Louise Bright, and Miss Lydia Bright." Then she emphasized, "They are friends of my aunt, Lady Bloomfield." Sophia made it obvious that she was disowning their friendship. She would never claim them as friends again. "This is Mr. Huntley, my fiancé," she finished grudgingly.

Sophia kept her mouth clamped shut after that. She was angry and could hardly trust herself to speak. But as the conversation continued among the others, she became angrier still. Mr. Huntley seemed far too congenial.

"Quite an early arrival to summer we're having, isn't it? Usually the only way we know summer has arrived is that the rain is warmer."

Louise and Lydia still didn't speak, but Mrs. Bright was perfectly willing to chat now that Mr. Huntley was present, although she was still a bit snippy in her reply. "The warmth is unlikely to last, but as I told my girls before we left this morning, we need to take advantage of the few nice days we have."

Mr. Huntley and Mrs. Bright chatted for several minutes while Sophia ground her teeth at his polite, friendly tone. Was he not offended at all by Mrs. Bright's rudeness? The conversation moved from the weather to the next ball they would all meet at; it was maddening!

They couldn't stay stopped on the path for long. Within a few moments, good-byes were said, although Sophia remained indignantly silent.

But that only lasted until the Brights' carriage was out of ear-shot. "They weren't even going to acknowledge me," she cried. "That was the rudest behavior I have ever witnessed." She darted an angry glance back at the departing carriage, then urged her horse faster in the opposite direction. "I hope I never meet the Brights again. What ball were you talking about with them? I must make sure I don't attend."

Mr. Huntley was still much too complacent. "Miss Spencer, surely their reaction isn't a surprise. They must have heard that our wedding didn't take place and thought the worst about you. Unless everyone knows we are married or about to be married, then your reputation is in shreds."

"You know, I'm beginning to hate that word." Mr. Huntley looked at her questioningly, and she almost growled. "Reputation," she said and let out a frustrated breath through her teeth. "It has far too much false importance—just like that awful Mrs. Bright and her awful daughters."

After a pause, Mr. Huntley said, "I shall have to stay near you whenever we are out to avoid another scene like that one."

Sophia was aghast. "We have to be together every moment?" she asked with distaste apparent in her voice.

She didn't realize how that must sound to Mr. Huntley until he quietly asked, "Is my company really so unpleasant, Miss Spencer?"

Sophia didn't answer right away, noticing that it was "Miss Spencer" again and not "Sophia."

Mr. Huntley looked as though he regretted the question and was about to say something else, perhaps brush the whole inci-dent aside. Sophia's conscience wouldn't allow that, so she quickly cleared her throat. "I don't mind your company," she said. Then releasing another angry sigh, she went on, "I'm angry at them. Not just the Brights, but all of them." She pushed her hand at the space behind her, indicating the vast park full of people. "I'm angry at them for forcing us into this predicament. It's so frustrating that my choices keep getting taken away from me." Saying it out loud made it seem even more true. Her father had never imposed strict rules on her, and she loved that freedom. She just didn't realize how much until she didn't have it anymore. "To find that I can't even step away from you or I'll be treated like I've just escaped from a leper colony . . . well, it's just not fair."

Mr. Huntley gave her a long, contemplating look before answering. "You're right. It's not fair." Then he looked away as he spoke. "About five years ago, my father died, and he left me with many burdens. For a time, all I could think about was how I didn't deserve it. It seemed like everyone had abandoned me. Most of my father's tenants and servants left, my friends became scarce, and even my mother moved away. She went to a neighboring county to live with my sister and her young family." He shrugged in a self-deprecating way. "Everyone seeing you as an object to avoid—I know that feeling."

Sophia stared down at her horse's mane. Her cheeks were now flushed with embarrassment rather than anger. "How awful," she murmured shamefully.

"Yes, it was awful," Mr. Huntley continued, "and I had pretty much decided to give up when Charles came to see me." He paused, probably remembering the details. Sophia was surprised to see a nostalgic smile appear on his face. "He acted as though nothing was wrong. In fact, he almost seemed excited for me, saying, 'What an opportunity to prove what you're capable of,' and, 'Once things turn around, you'll look back on this and laugh.'" He chuckled a little at the memory of it. "I still can't believe he was right. Things are much better now, but I have become cynical of society and its hypocrisy. Charles and Lucy have tried to keep me from being bitter, but I haven't always let them." He cleared his throat self-consciously. "I'm sure you can avoid the pitfalls of life that have so easily brought me down. You seem strong—much stronger than I first gave you credit for. I suppose I'm trying to say that even though it's not fair, I hope you won't end up feeling resentful," he concluded. Then he tagged on, "Especially toward me."

This caused Sophia to smile just a little. She rolled her eyes at him and said sarcastically, "Of course I could never resent *you*." Then she turned and looked him in the eye. "Thank you for sharing that with me," she said sincerely. "I won't let them win. I won't let them make me bitter. After all, it's just a few weeks. Then I'll leave all my problems in London and everything will go back to the way it was before."

For some reason, Mr. Huntley nodded vaguely and looked away.

Sophia took that opportunity to observe him. She was surprised to realize that she didn't feel any ill will toward him now. She had told him yesterday that she accepted his apology; however, she still felt that she had been unfairly treated. But his honest confession about his past caused her to feel remorse for going on and on about how unjust the situation was for her.

His stiff, awkward manner that morning helped her forgive him too. He had been so nervous speaking to her at first. His hesitant approach, more than anything else, helped her to forget his behavior from yesterday. She couldn't help but smile as she thought of it again. He turned back to her and caught her smiling at him. Sophia quickly turned it into a bland smile and looked off in the distance. She hoped he wasn't observing her profile, because he surely wouldn't miss her blush.

Seventeen

Returning to Dalton House, Alex dismounted and then helped Miss Spencer down from her horse. He enjoyed the sensation of holding her hand even though it was for only a brief moment. Before he could bid her farewell, a carriage arrived. The driver pulled up to the door just behind them, and Lady Anne and another lady emerged from the carriage. Lady Anne immediately spotted Miss Spencer and Alex, walked over to them, and asked, "Did you have a nice time?"

Alex could see the expression on Miss Spencer's face and guessed that she was about to tell Lady Anne all about her run-in with the Brights. Not wanting Lady Anne to think he hadn't fulfilled his part of the plan, Alex quickly answered. "On a day like this, how could we not?"

Luckily, Miss Spencer didn't get a chance to contradict him. "Yes, it is a lovely day," Lady Anne responded absently. Then she turned and called her friend over. "Mrs. Sutter, this is Mr. Huntley and Miss Spencer," she said, making introductions, "who I've just been telling you all about." With just a brief pause for breath, she then said, "Mr. Huntley, Sophia, this is Mrs. Sutter, a dear friend of mine and a lady who is sympathetic to your current troubles. She and I have been talking over the sad business this morning, and she has an excellent idea to turn the tide of public opinion in your favor."

Miss Spencer narrowed her eyes at Mrs. Sutter, and Alex felt that his expression probably matched her distrustful look. Alex didn't want to be part of any more schemes. "I'm just leaving," he said, "but it was nice to have met you, Mrs. Sutter." He shifted the reins to his other hand as he prepared to mount his horse.

"Mr. Huntley, don't leave yet," Lady Anne quickly said. "You haven't even heard what we're planning. You must come inside and join us for tea."

He tried to politely decline the invitation but was immediately overridden by Lady Anne, who took the reins from his hands and handed them over to her driver. She assured Alex that the horses would be well looked after in the stable.

Lady Anne led the group to the parlor and gave instructions to the housekeeper that tea should be served as soon as possible. "Now," she addressed them, "you must hear all about what Mrs. Sutter and I have planned."

Alex was not keen to be involved in another plan. He still wasn't sure about Lady Anne's last plan. Especially after today, misleading Miss Spencer just didn't feel right. Besides that, Mrs. Sutter seemed to personify the typical society matron who loved gossip, constantly pried into other peoples' affairs, and meddled beyond what one could bear.

Mrs. Sutter lost no time in sharing her idea. "A ball in your honor, Miss Spencer," she pronounced with satisfaction. "It's the very thing needed to bring you back into everyone's good graces."

Alex disagreed completely. After her disastrous ride in the

park this morning, he was sure that a ball singling out Miss Spencer would surely be considered presumptuous. Alex was about to politely decline her help, but Mrs. Sutter didn't wait for any dissenting opinions. "Lord and Lady Fitzgerald will host the ball, and we'll put on the invitations that it is being held in honor of your recent come-out. That will show Lady Bloomfield just how backward she was in not giving a come-out ball for you herself."

Alex glanced at Miss Spencer, who looked surprised by this opinionated woman. Perhaps that was what helped her to find her voice.

"Please, I don't want to do anything to hurt my aunt. She was so kind to host me for the Season. I feel already as though I've completely let her down. I don't want to make matters worse by embarrassing her further."

Alex was surprised to hear Miss Spencer defend her aunt. Did she still not realize that Lady Bloomfield was to blame? Despite this, Alex was impressed that Miss Spencer was standing up to Mrs. Sutter. She really did have a stronger character than he had given her credit for. But Mrs. Sutter and Lady Anne were ready to override any objection.

"We could call it an engagement ball if you would prefer, Sophia," Lady Anne said. "Although, I'm not sure why you want to defend your aunt. She has been very remiss with you." Mrs. Sutter voiced the same opinion and started in on a long and persuasive argument in favor of the ball.

Alex was curious how Miss Spencer would handle such pressure and was once more impressed with her response. "I don't want to have a come-out ball, or an engagement ball, or any kind of ball. I hope you won't think of me as ungrateful, but I have no desire to embarrass my aunt. I would like to draw as little attention to myself as possible."

Mrs. Sutter looked annoyed and Lady Anne disappointed, but Miss Spencer stood and took her leave. Alex quickly followed after her as she made her way out the terrace door and down the steps to the back garden.

∽⌽∾

Sophia didn't realize that Mr. Huntley was following her until she reached the hedge at the back of the garden. She turned and saw him, and his steps slowed as he approached her. Sophia waited for him to speak.

"I need to apologize to you, Miss Spencer."

Miss Spencer was surprised. Mrs. Sutter's and Lady Anne's attempt to help their situation certainly wasn't his fault. "No, you really don't. You've apologized enough for losing your temper. Let's think no more about it." She began walking along the path, and he matched his pace to hers.

"Well, I was actually going to say how sorry I am for coming between you and your aunt. It's obvious from what you said back there that being at odds with her is upsetting to you. It was because of my awful temper you left the wedding, but you are the one she is angry at."

Sophia was dismissive of his apology. "You don't need to apologize for that. This is my first time in London. I only met my aunt a few weeks ago."

"Oh." Mr. Huntley thought for a moment, a puzzled expression on his face. "It's strange that we even met," he finally said.

"Why do you say that?" Sophia asked.

"It just strikes me as odd—the unlikely circumstances that brought us together. It's your first time in London, and this is my first time back to London in more than five years."

She sighed. "Why did you come back now?" She cringed a little at the accusation she heard in her own voice, but Mr. Huntley answered her as if he hadn't noticed.

"I came to settle some affairs with the bank for Boxwell Court."

"Is that where you live?"

"Yes, Boxwell Court is my home. It's in Gloucestershire." She wondered if Boxwell Court was as grand as its name and if there was a stable full of horses. Sophia couldn't bring herself to ask the question, though. She didn't want Mr. Huntley to hear the curiosity in her voice.

Luckily for her, Mr. Huntley continued on the subject. "Boxwell Court got its name from all the boxwood trees. We used to have acres and acres of them. My father sold them all for timber a few years before he died. They're just now growing back. Not as many as before, though. Part of the land has been used for crops." Mr. Huntley suddenly shook his head in self-derision. "I'm sorry, Miss Spencer. Of course you don't want to hear about crops and trees and Boxwell Court."

"No, I don't mind at all," she said. Then, realizing she had said it too eagerly, she tried to tone her voice down. "Er, it's fine, I haven't traveled much, and it is always interesting to hear about new places. Besides, I don't want to go back inside until Mrs. Sutter has gone."

Mr. Huntley smiled. "I don't blame you. But you handled her so well. I can't believe I ever thought you were weak willed. If you don't mind me asking, why were you able to stand up to her so easily, but not your aunt?"

"I'm not sure." Sophia thought for a moment before responding. "It wasn't easy to tell Mrs. Sutter no, but she had a straightforward request: she wanted a ball. I don't. But my aunt was much more clever than her, always saying things in a way that I couldn't contradict.

"While I was with my aunt, I was trying so hard to . . . not stand out. But I think I've realized that I'd rather just be myself, even if it means not being accepted. And, of course, more than anyone else, I wanted my aunt to like me. I know that will never happen now, but there is no reason to make her hate me more than she does already by letting the Fitzgeralds give a ball in my honor."

Mr. Huntley didn't look too happy at this admission. "Are you saying you don't want a ball just for Lady Bloomfield's sake?"

Sophia gave Mr. Huntley a significant look. "No," she said, drawing the word out. "I mostly don't want a ball because the last one I attended put me off of balls—possibly for life."

Mr. Huntley seemed surprised at her jest and smiled at her. "Ah, yes. I understand the sentiment."

They had taken a full turn around the garden, but Sophia declined returning inside just yet. Mr. Huntley led her to a bench, and they sat down together.

Sophia wanted to hear more about Boxwell Court and how Mr. Huntley had worked to save it, but she didn't want to seem too interested, knowing that it could be misconstrued. Continuing on the subject of balls might be safe, though, so she asked, "Do you ever hold balls at Boxwell Court?"

"No, definitely not." Then, looking almost apologetic for being too adamant, he added, "We used to, of course. When I was younger, and my mother and sisters were there to plan them, we had balls and house parties and such." He was silent, likely reminiscing for a moment. "I'm the only one there now, so most of the house is shut."

He didn't go on, so Sophia asked, "Is that so?" just to keep him talking.

He nodded. "It's nothing like it used to be. There used to be so much commotion. Not just myself and my sisters—we had cousins who would come stay for the summer, where we got into endless mischief with. Every memory from my youth at Boxwell Court is a happy one."

Sophia smiled at such a sentiment. She, too, had enjoyed a happy childhood. Being an adult was proving to be much more complicated.

She could tell that Mr. Huntley's thoughts reflected hers when he said, "Too bad those happy times had to end. I have to look at Boxwell Court as a source of income now. I spend all my time pouring over the accounts, trying to find ways to squeeze another farthing out of the place. And I've hardly seen my relatives in the last five years."

Mr. Huntley suddenly seemed to remember who he was talking to and quickly shook off the melancholy mood. "But the house is still magnificent," he said in a much more positive voice. "It faces east, but my favorite view is when I'm returning from the west fields when the sun is going down. It's quite a picture, the way it sits on the hill just so." He gestured with his hands, and his shoulder brushed against Sophia's. Until then she hadn't realized how close they were sitting together. Mr. Huntley stopped talking and looked down at her. He hadn't pulled away, though.

His shoulder felt so strong and substantial against hers.

Sophia realized that Mr. Huntley had not only stopped talking, but had also stopped moving altogether. Not knowing how to react, she froze too. Several moments passed in silence, and she heard only the sound of her breathing.

But the dazed feeling didn't last too long. As Sophia recovered her senses, she leaned away from him to break the physical connection. Her eyes were still locked with Mr. Huntley's, but he looked quite distracted, as though he was looking at her but thinking of something else. He was probably distracted by the scene of Boxwell Court he had just described to her. She turned away to break from his gaze, hoping he wouldn't notice the pink in her cheeks.

"Sounds beautiful," she said.

"Yes. Yes, it is," he replied, distracted again. Sophia glanced back and noticed that he was looking away from her to the back of the garden.

"Definitely worth saving," she said, hoping he would keep talking about it. But this time it didn't work. He gave her a tight smile and looked away again.

Sophia waited a few more moments, but Mr. Huntley maintained his silence. Sensing that he wasn't inclined for company anymore, she finally said, "I'm sure Mrs. Sutter has gone by now, so I'll return inside. Thank you again for our pleasant outing, Mr. Huntley." Sophia stood, and Mr. Huntley copied the action.

"The pleasure was mine, Miss Spencer."

⮑⮐

Alex stayed in the garden until the door shut behind Miss Spencer. He then made his way around the house to the stable to collect the horses. He thanked the groom who had taken care of them and rode back to the Evertons' house with his thoughts churning.

What had just happened to him? When his arm brushed against Miss Spencer, he wanted to quickly say "I'm sorry" and shift away so it wouldn't happen again. Instead, every thought had flown out of his head as he looked into her upturned face. She was much closer than he had realized, and her wide hazel eyes had captivated him. They had been so close that the distance could have been easily eliminated by leaning forward a few inches. He hadn't leaned forward, of course, but the thought of kissing her had consumed him, and he'd had to turn away, almost dizzy with the effort of resisting.

Luckily, he had resisted.

His goal was to prove what a gentleman he was so that he could convince Miss Spencer to accept a real engagement. Today was almost a complete failure. He had been stiff and boring on their ride, and then after running into the Brights, he had practically preached her a sermon. Talking about Boxwell Court had been depressing, and after he thought about kissing her he couldn't talk at all. It was a disastrous performance, to say the least. He would have to do much better tomorrow.

He was surprised that he felt attracted to her. He had been so angry with her that the thought of being married to her caused him misery. But after one day spent in her company, he could see that he had misjudged her. She was quite pretty, but that alone didn't cast a spell over him. It was her character that attracted him. She was loyal and sweet—admirable traits in anyone, of course, but combined with her beauty, he was captivated.

Now if only he could captivate her in a similar way. He felt sure this would be an easier task if she had never seen him lose his temper so completely. Despite the extra trouble it had caused, getting all the built-up anger out of his system had been beneficial. If he had still been holding onto it, he wouldn't have seen her fine qualities. The situation still wasn't a favorable one, but now that his anger had been dispersed, he was discovering that Miss Spencer wasn't so bad after all.

Eighteen

The next evening, Alex followed Lord and Lady Fitzgerald into the Ashbys' vast ballroom with Miss Spencer at his side. The gown she was wearing was a light shade of green. And although he wasn't one to typically notice such things, he couldn't help but think that the lovely color perfectly accentuated her complexion. She must have felt his eyes on her because she glanced over at him. When their eyes met, she smiled, and he again felt a desire to kiss her. He looked away as soon as he could and tried to distract himself by looking around the room.

The Ashbys had arranged their ballroom for the musical trio's performance with a stage at the front and plenty of space for a large audience. Alex prepared to enjoy himself. He had always loved an evening of music. Of course, when he was young and wanted to perpetuate his reckless reputation, he never would have admitted it, but it was much more enjoyable for him than any other entertainment. He was anticipating Miss Spencer's reaction as well. The previous day, on their ride, she had mentioned that she enjoyed music and played a little. But this would be the real test. Alex still remembered sitting at a concert with Miss Towler, who had professed to love music, but after the first song or two, she couldn't stop fidgeting and yawning. He truly hoped that the music would be excellent and that Miss Spencer would enjoy it as much as he would. He could already tell that Miss Spencer had a far superior character to Miss Towler. And although it had been five years since he had seen Miss Towler, he knew that Miss Spencer was more beautiful too.

Alex looked up as the crowd began to hush, signaling that the performance was about to begin. His breath caught in his chest and his heart raced as he recognized the very woman he had just been comparing to Miss Spencer, the woman who had betrayed him at his lowest point—Miss Harriet Towler. She was on the arm of Lord Ashby as he gave a little speech of welcome to his guests and introduction of the renowned musicians they were about to hear.

Of course, Alex thought. *Miss Harriet Towler is now Lady Harriet Ashby.* He had never heard that she had married, but he should have assumed that her father would find her a suitable match. Lord Ashby had wealth and a title, two things that Alex hadn't possessed when he had tried to marry the young Miss Towler—two things that he still didn't possess. But Alex couldn't help but notice that Lord Ashby was also at least fifteen years older than him.

Miss Spencer must have noticed his startled reaction because she leaned over and whispered, "Are you well?"

This brought Alex back to the present, and he made an effort to appear as himself. "Yes," he replied, forcing a smile. "I've just seen someone I recognized from years ago, and it surprised me." Then, to avoid any questions on the matter, he asked, "Are you comfortable, Miss Spencer? You're not sitting in a draft, are you?"

The performance began before Miss Spencer could respond. Despite dreading a confrontation with Harriet, Alex enjoyed the trio, which was superb. He was also relieved to see Miss Spencer's rapt attention to the moving music. It was nice to have something in common with her.

During a short pause, she leaned toward him and said, "I'm not sure how I'll go back to the old music socials in Tissington after this." It reminded Alex how he needed to convince her not to return to Tissington at all, but rather to accompany him to Boxwell Court as his bride. He had a long way to go.

It was a shame, but the music couldn't last forever. When it was over, Alex knew he would have to face Harriet. He seriously hoped she had changed, because when they had been friends, she had loved to provoke others until they felt uncomfortable, creating awkward situations. He was ashamed of it now, but at the time, he had found it diverting.

Lord and Lady Ashby stationed themselves where they could greet all the guests as they passed into the drawing room, where refreshments were laid out. As Alex approached with Miss Spencer, Harriet looked directly at him. She had obviously already seen him, because she didn't look surprised at all to be meeting him now. Alex looked back and forth between Harriet and Lord Ashby, wondering what was about to happen and dreading it.

Before Harriet could speak, Lord Ashby said, "We are so pleased to have you with us this evening, Mr. Huntley." Then he continued, speaking a little quieter so as not to be overheard. "I know there's a little history between you and my wife, but I hope we won't have any unpleasant scenes because of it."

Alex was grateful to Lord Ashby for acknowledging it so frankly and downplaying the importance of the past. "Thank you, Lord Ashby. After such a splendid performance, an unpleasant scene is the furthest thing from my mind." Then, turning toward

Harriet, he uttered trite phrases of old friends meeting again in an attempt to diminish the importance of their shared past. "So nice to see you again, Lady Ashby. You are looking well. We'll have to catch up sometime."

But Alex could tell from the glint in her eye that she would not let him go so easily. "Alex, I heard you were getting married. Is this your *wife*, then?" By the way she emphasized the word *wife*, it was obvious that she had heard the gossip about the wedding that didn't happen.

Lord Ashby had moved away to speak to a guest who seemed to need him in another part of the room. Alex saw that Harriet was going to embarrass him and Miss Spencer intentionally, but he didn't quite know how to stop her. "Ah . . . no, this is my fiancée, Miss Spencer." He turned and said, "Miss Spencer, this is an old friend of mine, Lady Ashby."

"Not very chivalrous of you, Alex, to refer to me as your *old* friend." Harriet's voice was a little louder now that Lord Ashby wasn't nearby. A light smirk touched her lips.

Miss Spencer's eyes had been darting back and forth between Alex and Harriet through their short conversation. But now she seemed relaxed and confident. "How do you do," she said with narrowed eyes and a smirk of her own, followed by a slight inclination of her head. Alex's eyes widened. It was so subtle, but with that simple movement and her manner, Miss Spencer became the superior of the two.

Harriet could see as easily as Alex that Miss Spencer had the advantage, and she tried to reclaim it. "I had heard that you were to be married the other day. So what happened then, Miss Spencer? Did you jilt Alex too?"

He didn't let it show outwardly, but the words hurt and embarrassed Alex, just as Harriet had intended. He wondered at her lack of feeling. How could she not feel just as hurt and embarrassed by remembering what she had done to him? He knew he had changed since they parted, but had he ever really been as badly behaved?

In her guileless way, Miss Spencer responded, "No, Alex and I have just postponed the wedding." She wore a confident smile on her face that showed Lady Ashby had no power over her.

Harriet looked slightly put out that she had been unable to get a rise out of Miss Spencer, but she quickly regrouped and turned her attention back to Alex. "Alex, it seems your skills as a fortune hunter have worsened over the years. You used to be so selective. Now, obviously, anyone will do."

Alex again strove to keep his outward calm, but the insult to Miss Spencer provoked him just as Harriet had intended it to. "Harriet, the only thing that you ever had in your favor was your fortune," he replied, keeping his voice low. "And if I were you, I wouldn't start a conversation comparing yourself to Miss Spencer."

And before Harriet could find a cruel reply, Miss Spencer quickly added, "We're actually quite similar, Lady Ashby. We've both been fortunate enough to find men who accept us despite our faults." As she said this she gestured with her head to Lord Ashby, who was making his way back. Harriet turned and watched her husband as he made his way toward her. She looked back at Miss Spencer with an annoyed expression. But before Harriet could hiss out a comment, Miss Spencer turned to Alex. "Could we meet the musicians now?" she asked in a bright voice. "I'm so interested to find out the origin of the third concerto they performed."

It was so easily done. With a mere "Good evening, Lady Ashby," they were both away before Harriet could say anything else to offend them.

"Well done. Thank you for getting us away from her," Alex whispered as they moved into the adjoining room.

Miss Spencer nodded, acknowledging the compliment, and then asked, "Was Lady Ashby's name Miss Towler before she married?"

Alex nodded. He knew that after that conversation he would have to explain his past to Miss Spencer. But if she knew the name Miss Towler, she must have heard the gossip about their botched elopement five years ago. Still, he was anxious for her to know the truth, so he steered her to a quiet corner.

"Yes, that's her. You've obviously heard that she and I were about to be married and then she called it off. But let me explain. She and I were friends, and after my father died, I proposed to her and she said yes. With nothing but debt to my name, we knew that her father wouldn't approve, so we planned an elopement. I felt that it was love or close enough to it, but she obviously didn't. She told her father about the elopement, and that was the end of it."

Miss Spencer looked as if she didn't believe that the story ended there and raised her eyebrows in question.

"The story that I was a fortune hunter spread quickly," Alex continued, "and with that humiliation, I left London." He grimaced as he said, "I felt the injustice of it all very keenly, but looking back now I can see that I probably wouldn't have proposed to Harriet if she hadn't had twenty thousand pounds. It's hard to admit, but I suppose I was a fortune hunter. Not a very good one, thank goodness, or I would now be stuck with her for a wife." He grimaced at the thought.

Miss Spencer tried to hide her giggle. "She reminds me of an acquaintance back home whom I've frequently had to deal with. I knew that if I didn't rise to her bait it would bother her more than anything else."

Alex was impressed and told her so. "She was awful, but you handled it superbly. Thank you for staying calm and not letting her upset you." Then, deciding to cause a little trouble of his own, he smiled and said, "By the way, *Sophia*, I noticed you called me Alex."

Sophia looked self-conscious, just like he knew she would. He was learning that she had a strong character, which included a strong sense of what was right and wrong.

"Did *you* just call *me* Sophia?" she asked a little defensively with an arched eyebrow. "Besides, you did it first in Hyde Park when the Brights were being so awful."

Alex was privately flattered that she had noticed and remembered. Sophia continued. "I had to use your Christian name because she did. It would have been strange if I had not."

"You know, you have a point. In order for us to keep up this charade, we should use our Christian names all the time."

Sophia looked taken aback at the suggestion and began, "I didn't mean—"

"That will make it very convincing that we intend to marry," Alex pressed, "don't you think?"

Sophia shrugged. "Are you sure it's allowed?" Then, with heavy irony in her voice, she added, "I'd hate to do something improper that might damage my reputation."

A surprised bark of laughter escaped before Alex could bring it down to a quiet chuckle. He looked around and noticed that several people were looking his way. Harriet, too, was watching them with a scowl on her face. Alex turned away from her, not caring at all what she thought. Sophia's ability to find humor in their situation made Alex feel lighter than he had in days. He turned back to Sophia and saw that her hand was over her mouth to stifle a giggle, obviously finding it funny that his loud laugh had called attention to themselves. With a grin, he said, "Yes, it's allowed. And don't forget, your reputation is under my protection now."

Nineteen

Lady Anne was a bit disappointed that her matchmaking efforts hadn't produced results by now. She really thought it wouldn't take more than a day or two for Mr. Huntley and Miss Spencer to declare their love, but when they were together, all she could gather from her close observation of the pair was polite formality. Mr. Huntley's composure never failed, which made him difficult to read. As for Sophia, she seemed to be taking the situation at face value, pretending Mr. Huntley was her fiancé when they were in company, but back at Dalton House, the pretext was gone, and she distanced herself from him. The surest sign that she wasn't falling in love were the references about leaving London that continued to come up in her conversation. Lady Anne needed to change that somehow.

She tried to think of a way to get them alone together. If she could trap Mr. Huntley and Sophia in a room together for an hour or two, surely they would fall in love and declare their feelings for each other.

Her own son, little William, had been trapped in the library for over an hour one day because of a broken door handle. In the end, two footmen had taken the door off its hinges to rescue him. Unfortunately, the library door had been quickly repaired. Lady Anne checked to see if the door handle could possibly be broken again, but the repair work had been had been drattedly masterful. Besides, she couldn't think of any reason to lure them into the library. When visitors called at Dalton House, they were always received in the downstairs drawing room. There wasn't any viable reason for Mr. Huntley or Sophia to go upstairs to the library, and certainly no reason why they should both go up there together and shut the door.

By the time Mr. Huntley came to call the morning after the musicale, Lady Anne had given up on the plan. But observing the pair of them, she became determined once again. Mr. Huntley was trying to engage Sophia in conversation, but his manner was stiff. Each time he asked her a question, Sophia would answer with friendly politeness, but they always reverted to uncomfortable silence. It was only a week and a half until they would leave London, and at this slow pace, it would take them a year and a half to fall in love. They needed to be hurried along.

Again it was little William who helped her form a plan, but this time a much simpler one. After she had been sitting with Sophia and Mr. Huntley for five minutes, he came running into the room. He regularly came looking for Sophia whenever he managed to escape from his nursemaid.

Sophia pulled William onto her lap and bounced him on her knees for a few minutes while they waited for his nursemaid to catch up to him and take him away with all the usual apologies for the disruption. That was when Lady Anne saw an opportunity to leave them alone, and she took it. "William," she said to him, standing abruptly, "time to go back to the nursery." It was as good an excuse as any to leave the two alone together.

This was a change from the usual, and William was reluctant to leave until Sophia promised him, "If you go with your mother, I'll come up to the nursery and sing to you before bed again this evening." And William and his mother left the room, both feeling that they had gotten their way.

Lady Anne took William back upstairs to the nursery and spent a rare morning there with her children. She wasn't sure how much progress Alex and Sophia would make, but simply leaving them alone had been the best she could manage.

Sophia let her indulgent gaze follow William from the room. When she turned back to Alex, she found him regarding her with a curious expression on his face. Wondering what his thoughts were produced a curious expression of her own, and that's when Alex seemed to recollect himself. He blinked several times.

"How do you have such a natural ability with children?" he asked. His look was still perplexed as he continued, "With just your father for company, I would have thought you wouldn't have any experience in dealing with young children at all."

Sophia shrugged, not knowing how to answer. After thinking about it for a moment, she said, "My only experience with children is from when I would help father when he called on his patients. I would look after children whose parents were ill, or if his patient was a child, I would try to distract the child." With a slight cringe at the memory, she confessed, "At the time, I hated it." Sophia again paused in thought, remembering how she would walk up and down trying to calm a crying baby while his mother was being ministered to. "You see this scar?" she asked, pushing up her sleeve to her elbow. "This is where I cut myself on a shelf while I was trying to hold onto a little boy who was crying for his mother and trying to get away from me."

Alex moved over to the sofa where Sophia was sitting to get a closer look. He winced a little at the raised line of skin where there had once been an inch-long gash.

"Luckily, my father was there and sewed me right up. But I never enjoyed looking after children, and after this injury I refused to go along with him anymore."

"How old were you?"

"I was fifteen."

"I wonder why it's different now. You're nineteen, correct?" Sophia nodded, and Alex went on, "You were very sweet with little William just now. Why is that?"

Sophia paused again before answering. In their short acquaintance, this had already happened several times with Alex; he would ask her a question that would cause her to truly think. She felt as if she was getting to know herself as much as Alex was. "Well . . . perhaps because it's my choice now." It almost sounded like a question itself, but Sophia felt it was true. "When I'm forced to do something, I can't put my heart into it. But when I choose for myself, I give all of me," she said more confidently. It suddenly seemed an intimate thing to say. Alex was sitting close to her and peering at her with his clear blue eyes. She thought they must reflect how she felt. She broke his gaze to look away self-consciously.

She convinced herself that the closeness she felt was just in her imagination, and she was about to face Alex with a look of indifference when she felt his fingers lightly brush her small scar. Waves of sensation coursed through her. Her heart sped and her breath turned shallow, all from the lightest touch on her exposed arm.

His voice resonated as he said, "Perhaps that is why little William loves you so; because you give all of yourself when you are with him." Sophia's mind didn't even process the words he was saying. All she could think about was his finger gently tracing circles on her arm. She swallowed nervously as she watched his hand move. Then she slowly lifted her eyes to meet his. She froze under his intense gaze. It was difficult to draw breath. Alex's eyes searched hers while his hand stopped its gentle stroke and his grip became a bit firmer. Sophia's mind was in a haze, and it took her a moment to realize that Alex was pulling her gently closer to himself as he leaned toward her. He was so close that she felt his warm breath on her cheek, and that finally brought her to her senses.

She quickly turned her face away, but a quick glance back at Alex showed a look of dismayed surprise, as if he couldn't believe what had just happened. Sophia tried to regain her composure and bring their conversation back to solid footing. "William is a . . . is a very good little boy . . . it's probably nothing to do with me, just his own sweet nature." She pulled her arm out of his grasp as she spoke and rubbed her own hand where his had been to try to dispel the sensation. Another glance at Alex showed his features composed without any hint of discomfort.

She quickly turned their conversation away from herself by asking about his family. He seemed pleased to move onto a lighter topic as well. After she asked a question or two, he took the opportunity to describe them in detail. In telling her about his mother and his sisters and their families, he admitted to Sophia that he missed them and hoped to be closer to them in the future.

By the time he left, Sophia was feeling unsettled and, somehow, discontent. That near kiss had possibly been imagined. She had been caught up in a moment of attraction was all. But talking about children and her ability with them and listening to Alex describe his family had left her with longing. She had already made a choice to live with her ruined reputation. She knew that meant no husband or children for her. As she had sprinted away from Saint Luke's, she'd felt relieved by the prospect. Now doubt began to creep in. In her heart, she still wanted her future to include a happy family.

ﻗﻌﻭ

Several days later, Sophia was still feeling resentful toward Aunt Nora for her lack of help during her crisis. But she couldn't help feeling that Aunt Nora *had* actually protected her from making social gaffes.

Just yesterday, when she was walking up the street with Mr. Huntley to return to the Fitzgeralds' carriage, she had caught sight of a beautiful fur-lined cloak in a shop window. She had stopped and admired it—it was truly a most gorgeous cloak—but she didn't need a new cloak, so she said as much and continued walking. But not before catching an incredulous look from Mr. Huntley.

Somehow, admiring a cloak but not buying it was just not done. Aunt Nora certainly had her faults, but she had prevented Sophia from making mistakes like that in public.

Today, Sophia had been invited to dine with the Evertons, and she was nervous. Lord and Lady Fitzgerald would not be coming with her, having had a previous engagement to dine with one of Lord Fitzgerald's associates. Although they told Sophia she would be welcome to come along, they encouraged her to go to the Evertons without them. She would be on her own, without Lady Anne or even Aunt Nora to prevent her from making a spectacle of herself.

Sophia had never worried much about how others viewed her. But looking over her very short history with the Evertons, she realized they must have a low opinion of her. Falling asleep at their ball and being dragged away by her aunt was bad enough, but running away from the wedding afterward was sure to make them think that she was a jittery, nervous girl.

Alex spoke very highly of them, and from his description she thought they would have been her friends in better circumstances. She was determined to at least leave them with a better impression this time. She would be on her best behavior and she took extra care with her appearance. She chose one of her gowns from home that she had purchased before coming to London. She was worried that the Evertons might think less of her because it wasn't the latest style; she knew that it suited her much better than any of her new gowns. The cream-colored gown with a darker cream sash was simple, yet Sophia felt elegant when she wore it. She would need that confidence today.

The Evertons' butler opened the door for her, and Sophia smoothed her hair before stepping into their vast entrance hall. She immediately recalled the events from just over a week ago. What a disaster the Evertons' ball had been for her and Alex. It was unlikely she'd ever forget it. Returning to the place of her disgrace made her feel even more nervous.

Alex came to greet her almost immediately. For just a moment she felt more nervous than ever, but then Alex smiled, and she felt herself relax.

Sophia smiled back, happy to see him. They both stood there smiling, and Sophia briefly wondered if she should say something so it wouldn't feel awkward, but then she caught the warm look in Alex's eyes and forgot to wonder about it anymore.

"Hello, Sophia," Alex said so quietly that it felt like he was telling her a private secret. He took a step closer and she felt he was almost too close. She leaned her head back to look at him. She had the impression he was about to say something more, but then Lord and Lady Everton appeared.

Sophia's attention was immediately claimed by them, and her determination to win them over returned. She was struck by how young Lady Everton looked and wondered how long she had been married. Sophia thought they must be quite near the same age. As they were reintroduced, she offered her most formal "how do you do." However, all her efforts to impress them with her fine manners were immediately thwarted when Lady Everton returned her greeting. "I do hope you will call us Charles and Lucy—if you can forgive us, that is. We feel so terrible about what happened. I'm surprised you even came here today, but it gives me hope. I truly want you to forgive us, and I hope we can be friends."

Sophia was taken aback by the friendliness and apology from Lady Everton, and an ironic laugh escaped her. "I was going to beg for your forgiveness, for being such an imbecile—"

"No, no, I won't allow you to apologize," Lucy interrupted. "It all happened through no fault of your own. I am just so deeply ashamed that I didn't notice what was happening and put a stop to it somehow." She pulled Sophia's arm through hers as they walked to the dining hall, another gesture of informality that Sophia found she liked.

"Of course it's not your fault, Lady Everto . . . I mean, Lucy. It was just an accident that all of us would have prevented if we could."

Lucy turned back and exchanged a guilty expression with Charles and Alex. "Well, that isn't entirely true. We have been questioning the servants to see if we could find out what went wrong that night, and at first nothing came of it. But then, yesterday, one of the housemaids overheard our scullery maids talking, and one of them boasted about how she knew the whole house because she was so good at sneaking around. Well, when the housekeeper began to question her about this 'sneaking around' and specifically about what happened at the ball and whether she knew which room was Alex's and if she had told anyone . . . she got flustered and left."

"We've been trying to find her," Charles said, taking up the explanation, "so we can get to the bottom of this, but we're not likely to. We suspect that she knew which room was Alex's and made sure that was where your aunt took you that night."

It didn't take Sophia long to catch on. She looked over at Alex, who appeared to have already heard about this latest development. "So you think someone intentionally wanted us to be found together? Not an accident, then?" Sophia was smart, but she was not naturally suspicious; she had never had a reason to be so. Her thoughts took a different turn, and she said, "I wonder if my aunt knows that someone deliberately told her the wrong room? Maybe she won't be so frustrated with me when she hears it wasn't an accident after all." Sophia lost hope for that as she recalled the rest. "Actually, she'll never forgive me for running away from the wedding, so I suppose it doesn't really matter."

Lucy looked thoughtful and tentatively asked, "Sophia, how close are you and your aunt?"

"I had never met her until I came to London a few weeks ago, although we had exchanged several letters to arrange my visit. I thought we would become close, but . . ." Sophia trailed off with a shrug and a shake of her head.

Lucy glanced at Alex and Charles. "Don't you think your aunt may have planned it? Maybe she's the one who wanted you disgraced."

Sophia thought for a moment before answering. She remembered several instances before Charles's and Lucy's ball when she had suspected that Aunt Nora was annoyed or angry with her. It had caused Sophia to wonder if Aunt Nora was unhappy about the inheritance grandmother had left her. But even if she had been, there was no reason why she should force Sophia into marriage. That wouldn't solve anything.

"I don't think so," Sophia said, "She seemed . . . irritated with me over the whole thing. I think she was quite worried that my damaged reputation would reflect poorly on her. She seemed almost relieved when I decided to stay with the Fitzgeralds after the wedding. I don't think she likes me, but she wouldn't have anything to profit from my disgrace."

Lucy didn't look convinced, and glancing at Alex and Charles again, Sophia saw that they looked skeptical as well. So she reiterated, "Really, there was nothing she could have gained from such a plot. In fact, I think she felt that she was very ill-used."

"How could she think that?" Lucy asked with crease between her brows. "After you and Alex were discovered, she seemed so angry on your behalf."

"Well, she was doing me such a favor by chaperoning me for the Season. It seemed to me that I was in her debt, and then not only did I not repay her kindness, but I also brought her down in disgrace with me." Then with a note of sadness in her voice, Sophia said, "She definitely holds me responsible for what happened."

Lucy still didn't look convinced, but she agreed with Sophia's conclusion. "From what I can see, Lady Bloomfield certainly had nothing to gain from a marriage between you. And I think that she would not want her name in any way associated with a scandal, so perhaps you're right," she said, although her tone still implied some doubt. "I think it's unlikely that we'll ever know for sure why this happened."

The conversation moved on to other things, and they had a lovely afternoon getting acquainted. Lucy had a talent of running a home that always felt welcoming, and Charles had a gift for putting others at ease with his open manner. The four of them were soon laughing. Charles started it by telling anecdotes, but it wasn't long before the others joined in.

For Sophia, it was a welcome change to what she had experienced so far in London. All her outings with Aunt Nora had been in society that had effectively intimidated her. She was still friendly, but it was less natural for her because she was always aware of the unspoken rules. Her reluctance to talk openly was rapidly fading in Charles and Lucy's company, especially as she saw how relaxed and animated Alex was in their presence. She was gaining confidence in their friendship with each passing minute, and gaining confidence in Alex as well.

During their conversation, Sophia realized that Alex must have been speaking to the Evertons about her because Charles and Lucy were familiar with the few details of her life that she had told Alex. But they were also genuinely interested in the further details she could provide.

"Your father must be quite low to have his only daughter so far from home for so long. How is he surviving without you?" Lucy asked near the end of dinner.

From his letters, it seemed that he was surviving just fine without Sophia. The last letter she had from him had arrived the day before the wedding (which he obviously had not heard of when he wrote). He had been busy with work. The impression she got was that he was devoting himself to his patients while Sophia was gone. He had expressed, however, that he missed her and would be happy to see her home again. But for Sophia, after everything that had happened to her, she was missing her father more than she thought she ever would.

Sophia was sure her voice wouldn't remain steady if she answered Lucy's question seriously, so she made a joke of it instead. "I am sure it is a huge relief to him to be spared giving me lectures for these weeks I've been away. No one is more intent on improving me than my dear father."

Lucy looked pleasantly surprised by Sophia's admission. "He sounds just like my father," she exclaimed. "When he comes to visit, he still lectures me about not being a bad influence on Charles with my irreverent ways!"

"Actually, Lucy, I've been quite worried about that myself," Charles pronounced in a solemn voice.

Sophia giggled and Alex grinned broadly as Lucy sweetly

replied, "You shouldn't worry about that, my love. I've decided to influence you with an elbow to your ribs instead."

Charles, with a warm smile, replied, "In all honesty I don't know what your father sees. I don't think you can be improved upon; you *are* perfection."

It was proper and gallant for Charles to say that his wife was perfection, but Sophia sensed that for him, it was also the truth. She turned her gaze to Alex just as he turned and met hers. His light blue eyes seemed to hold a secret between the two of them, a private moment where something was conveyed without being said.

She wished for just a moment to be his perfection. But of course she wasn't. Once she left London with Lord and Lady Fitzgerald, he would be free from his duty to her. They had become friends, but she sensed that he was just making the best of a difficult situation.

As if to prove what she had been thinking, Alex asked in a friendly tone, "What about your father, Sophia? What does he lecture you to improve? Is it your natural tendencies he tries to correct, or do you intentionally provoke him?"

Sophia smiled mischievously. "Perhaps it began as a natural tendency, but when I discovered how to use it to get my way, my behavior became deliberate." In response to Alex's skeptical look, she went on, "I've discovered it is to my advantage to appear reluctant whenever I'm asked to serve or sacrifice, because my father will offer me rewards for tasks I would have done anyway."

Alex exhaled a disbelieving laugh. "I don't believe you. You seem far too unassuming for any such thing."

"I have to look innocent for the trick to work, of course," Sophia responded with an arch look. "And for my rewards I have received several new dresses, a new stall for my horse, and a day at the fair to name a few." The triumph in her voice turned to self-mockery. "Of course, the long speeches that went with the rewards made them hardly worth it, which is perhaps why I've stopped teasing my father so much."

With mock reprimand in his voice, Charles said, "Sophia, you shouldn't reveal so much with Alex here. You'll want to save all these mischievous deeds for when you are married, for I do believe wives try to pull the wool over their husbands' eyes as much as possible."

Sophia looked up sharply as Charles's words sank in. She gave Alex a questioning look. "I thought you said you told them?" she asked quietly. When Alex didn't immediately reply, and noting the guilty look that he couldn't quite suppress, a new suspicion began to form in her mind. The suspicion solidified as she saw Alex glare in Charles's direction.

Sophia also turned toward Charles, who was looking uncomfortable now.

"You mustn't mind what I said, Sophia," he said. "I just want to see Alex happy, and so I try to be a matchmaker for him."

Sophia acknowledged Charles's words with a smile, but it was forced. Her smile became more genuine, albeit reluctant, as she watched Lucy awkwardly lean out of her chair and elbow Charles in the ribs. It helped lighten the mood, but Sophia still suspected that she had somehow been excluded from Alex's plans.

The thought had crossed her mind that Alex had given up far too easily after she ran out on the wedding. His honor seemed vital to him, but he had never tried to persuade her to marry him. Perhaps because he was planning it all along without her consent.

Still conscious of a desire to leave the Evertons with a good impression, Sophia tried to not show how upset she was. But she felt humiliated and angry, and by the time the carriage was ordered for her, her anger had grown.

She hated the thought that she was being manipulated. Looking back on the last few weeks of her life, she could see that she had been manipulated over and over again.

Besides running away from the wedding, she hadn't made a single choice for herself. Everything had been decided for her. She had almost become used to it with Aunt Nora, who always brushed aside Sophia's opinion as unimportant. Aunt Nora had such a strong character she had overridden Sophia's will every time.

But to realize that Alex had excluded her from his plans, as though she were a willful child who had to be tricked into something unpleasant, she found it was more upsetting than when Aunt Nora had done it.

Twenty

Alex stood near the door, waiting as Sophia said good night to Charles and Lucy. Sophia had become quieter after Charles's unfortunate remark. He knew she had figured out his scheme. He supposed he had also become quieter. His mind was busily engaged in trying to find a way out of this new predicament.

Alex led her down the steps to the Evertons' carriage and held Sophia's hand as she stepped in and was disappointed when she let go so quickly. He was apprehensive as he stepped in and sat across from her, and rightly so. As soon as the door was shut, Sophia was ready to confront him.

"I agreed to a fake engagement. I never agreed to a real one," she immediately said.

Alex felt that the timing wasn't right; it was too soon. He had hoped to have at least another week in London with her. And although Sophia didn't know about it, he also planned on accompanying her and the Fitzgeralds back to Tissington so that he would have the three-day journey to convince her to change her mind about him.

Sophia was obviously angry, but he didn't have any other choice—he had to convince her now. "Sophia, let me explain." With only a slight hesitation and a deep breath to fortify him, he began, "After you left me standing at the altar, I was annoyed about the delay, but I had no doubt we would still marry."

Sophia let out an angry huff and crossed her arms in front of her. "You must think quite highly of yourself not to have taken it as a personal insult!" she exclaimed. Alex was conscious of what she was implying, and he knew he looked chagrined. He had better proceed with caution.

"Please let me explain?" Alex asked again.

She leaned back in her seat and gave him an angry and challenging stare, just daring him to explain it all to her satisfaction.

Though he was feeling nervous, he accepted the challenge. "When you ran away from the church, I was mostly annoyed at myself because I knew it was my fault for losing my temper with you, and I knew I would have to repair the damage. After receiving your note, I went to the Fitzgeralds' with the intention to convince you to come back to the church and marry me that day. When Lady Anne told me how little chance I had of persuading you to marry me so soon, I agreed to her plan: to act as if the engagement wasn't real and persuade you once you knew me better."

He saw Sophia's eyebrows rise in surprise, and then her eyes narrowed in anger again. He realized he had just given away Lady Anne's involvement in the plot, although if it would transfer some of the blame from him and help his cause, he wouldn't be too sorry for the slip. Still he tried to fix it by reminding Sophia of their earlier conversation. "You really can't blame us too much, Sophia. You yourself admitted that you've been guilty of the same thing."

She gave him a look of surprised innocence, so he explained, "You withheld information from your father so that he would reward you for things you meant to do anyway."

Sophia looked a little guilty but quickly tried to gain the righteous high ground again. "That's not the same thing! Children are forever trying to outwit their parents—it's to be expected!" As she spoke, she lifted her hands to her face as if to hide her blushing cheeks.

Alex was amused at her justification but knew that to laugh at that moment would end any hope he had of succeeding. Sophia did narrow her eyes a bit at the twitch of his lips, but he cleared his throat and said, "You're right. It's not the same. All I can do is tell you how sorry I am that I misled you and how much I hope you can forgive me."

Her indignation seemed to melt a little at that, but she didn't answer. Perhaps she was not ready to forgive him quite yet.

"As you now have realized," he continued, "each of our outings has been to publicly show that we are still engaged but also to convince you that I'm not such a villain after all." He knew that he needed to ask her now, but he was feeling uncertain what answer she would give. Sophia still looked angry, but Alex observed that she looked embarrassed too. It made him feel slightly better. He gently pulled one of her hands away from her flushed cheeks and held it in his own. "I wasn't thinking of marriage at all before I met you. I felt I had so many goals to reach before I could even begin to think about marriage. But since the night we met it has been constantly on my mind. At first I was unhappy about it—we both were. But every moment I spend with you, I realize it's not such a bad thing after all." Quickly realizing that he would have to do better than that, he said, "I think you and I will suit each other very well. Perhaps we should forget about blaming anyone for our predicament and just agree that this is what is supposed to happen."

Sophia was looking at him quite intently, as if trying to discern whether he meant it or not. But she hadn't said anything yet, and Alex was worried. "Sophia, can we please just agree to a real engagement?" he asked, knowing his hands clasped hers a bit too tightly.

But instead of giving him an answer, Sophia stared into his eyes for a long moment before asking, "Do you *want* to marry me, Alex?"

Alex wanted to reply, "What I want is irrelevant. We have to marry!" But he held the words in. This was a crucial moment, and he knew that bringing up the necessity of their marriage would only make matters worse. So he honestly assessed his thoughts: did he want to marry Sophia? These last few days as they had spent so much time together, he found that he enjoyed her company and even looked forward to seeing her. While waiting for her to arrive today at Charles's and Lucy's house, he had pulled out his watch every five minutes in anticipation.

Alex had noticed several times things about Sophia that might make her his perfect match. Of course she was beautiful and, in the right company, sociable and witty. But foremost in his mind was that she had been brought up with the highest manners, but not surrounded with abundance like the rest of the *ton*. There was evidence in this when she made subtle references to the modesty of her father's house and how it was managed, or turning away from a shop window rather than buying something she didn't need. Alex had thought more than once that since he had to take a wife, at least it was Sophia. Any other young lady would have been disastrous.

Up until a few weeks ago, Alex's sole purpose in life had been to restore his family estate. His thoughts had been centered on saving Boxwell Court for so long, and despite being extremely distracted since coming to London, they were still there, his entire focus. He had a huge obligation that was only half fulfilled.

So how to answer? Did he want to marry Sophia? If the necessity was taken away and he actually had a choice in the matter, is this what he would choose?

♾

Sophia didn't know what answer she was hoping for; she'd asked the question out of genuine curiosity. From everything Alex had said, it seemed that maybe he *did* want to marry her. She hadn't pinpointed her feelings yet, but she knew as soon as she asked the question that his answer could sway her feelings one way or the other.

After running away from the wedding, she had felt so determined to have a future of solitude. But just a taste of being an outcast had made her feel so rejected that she was less determined now. Sophia had also come to know Alex better, and everything she learned about him improved her impression. But perhaps that was inevitable; her first impression of him had been so low. His explanation was sufficient, she supposed, although not very romantic. But still, Sophia was almost convinced to agree to marry him. He wasn't awful as she had at first thought him to be, and agreeing to the marriage would put an end to the seemingly endless trouble about her reputation.

Alex still hadn't answered her question. Searching his face for clues, Sophia could see his hesitation. She waited for him to speak, but his silence was all the answer she needed: he obviously didn't want to marry her. She looked away in case there was disappointment in her eyes.

"Sophia," he began haltingly, "I've come to admire you very much—and there is no one else I'd rather marry than you." His words, so late in coming, were less than convincing. He was still holding something back. With a resigned sigh, he continued, "To be perfectly honest with you, the timing is wrong. I'm just not ready to take care of a wife yet. I told you how my father left me a legacy of burdens . . . I had hoped to have them all well behind me before taking on more. But if you are willing to put up with less than you deserve, I'm sure we can be happy together."

Alex's reason was an honorable one—she wouldn't expect anything less than that from him now—but it didn't satisfy Sophia. He hadn't said outright that he didn't want to marry her, but this was near enough. He had even referred to her as a burden. Perhaps other young ladies wouldn't mind being a burden to their husbands, but Sophia wanted to marry for love, as her parents had.

Maybe she shouldn't have such high expectations, but still she wanted *something*. She wanted to be more than an obligatory wife. But she also wanted be able to step into public without suffering shame and degradation. Really, she didn't know which to choose—they were both awful choices as far as she was concerned.

What she really wanted was her father. She had never appreciated before the protection he had provided. Aunt Nora had been vaguely insulting to her, Alex had yelled at her (just once, but it had been upsetting), the Brights had openly insulted her, and even Lady Anne had tried to arrange her marriage without her knowledge. She knew that her father would never have let any of that happen. She wanted to go back to Tissington and be with her father.

Sophia had been staring at her feet as these thoughts ran through her mind, but now she raised her eyes and said what was in her heart: "I want to go home." Alex looked at her blankly, which was not surprising since she had completely changed the subject. So she clarified, "I am so weary of being manipulated and . . . and pushed into making decisions I don't want. My father will know what I should do." She looked a bit accusatory as she said, "He might try to persuade me, but he will do so for my happiness and no one else's."

Sophia watched Alex let out a tense breath. "Of course. I should have thought of that myself. You want your father's advice. That's understandable." Alex was looking relieved as he leaned back and said, "I would like to meet your father and see where you are from, so I shall travel with you and the Fitzgeralds back to Tissington."

His reaction wasn't what Sophia had expected. Again, he had given in quite easily, without trying to persuade her to marry him. She tried to think of a reason why he would be relieved. Did he really not want to marry her and was grateful for a delay? Or did he think that with more time he could come up with another scheme to convince her? Sophia was starting to feel suspicious of everything, even small things like this. *And who could blame me?* she thought with asperity. Suspicion would quickly become natural to anyone who was the victim of as many plots as she had been.

They finished their carriage ride with Sophia watching Alex through narrowed eyes and Alex seemingly taking no notice whatsoever, looking to be on the verge of happiness.

Twenty-One

After the Evertons' carriage delivered her safely back at Dalton House, Sophia's thoughts wouldn't settle. The Fitzgeralds hadn't returned yet, and because she felt the need for solitude, Sophia decided to retire right away. She asked the butler if any letters had arrived for her, and the negative response increased the tense feeling that was building up inside her. Why hadn't her father written to her?

Sophia and her father hadn't ever been apart for so long, and with all she had gone through, she was missing him intensely. What's more, she hadn't received a letter from him this week. Since she arrived at Dalton House, she hadn't received any letters at all. She was anxious to hear his response to her most recent escapades. It was possible that Aunt Nora had received Sophia's correspondence and failed to forward it to her at the Fitzgeralds'. It was quite possible, really, considering Aunt Nora's unfriendliness toward her when she had called at Dalton house after the aborted wedding. Aunt Nora was probably very angry with her. Sophia hoped that by tomorrow she would hear from her father. Now that she had been at the Fitzgeralds' for over a week, she expected a letter from him soon.

She prepared for bed quickly and sent the maid on her way. Then she pulled the chair from her dressing table over to the window and stared out into the darkness. She couldn't see anything until she blew out her candle, but as she became accustomed to the darkness of the room, she could see the shapes of the trees outside her window. Thoughts of father and lost letters fled her mind, and she finally acknowledged to herself what was really troubling her.

Finding out tonight that Alex had intended their engagement to be real all along had come as quite a surprise, and she was just now realizing the implications. Ever since Alex turned up at the Fitzgeralds' after the wedding, he had been *pretending*.

Of course, they had both been pretending when there were others around. But now Sophia realized that even when it was just the two of them, Alex had been feigning his regard for her.

She didn't want to believe it, but he had tricked her by letting her think the engagement wasn't real. In what other ways had he tricked her? She had grown close to him that week; they had suffered the same injustices, and that had united them. But for Alex, had it all been an act?

The first time she saw him after running away from the wedding, he had apologized for being angry with her. Then there was their ride in the park, the concert at the Ashbys', and the two times he had called when he wasn't expected. Just remembering the look in his eyes when he had leaned toward her and she had thought he would kiss her caused her heart to speed up and her breath to hitch. Everything that had happened up to and including today's dinner at the Evertons—she couldn't help but wonder if it had all been part of a deception.

She had begun to feel something for Alex, just as he had intended her to. Each time she was in his company, her heartbeat sped up a little more than it had the time before. She wondered if it was all one-sided.

She tried to convince herself that some of those moments must have been sincere . . . but what if they weren't?

∽

As the carriage returned to the Evertons', Alex breathed another sigh of relief. Charles's slip at dinner had left him with an ever-so-delicate situation. Sophia wasn't ready to agree to a real engagement, but now that she knew the truth, he hadn't seen any other way to proceed but to push her into accepting the real thing. He was relieved that she had thought of a way for them to postpone the moment. He had been granted a reprieve. Sophia seemed to need more time to grow accustomed to this new state of things, but Alex felt confident she would come around. The next time the discussion of their marriage came up, he was certain she would finally agree. If nothing else, her father would surely insist on it, and since Sophia obviously relied on her father's advice, Alex was positive that within a month's time they would be wed.

Alex found Charles waiting for him in his library. He looked up from his book as Alex came in. "How much did my mistake cost you?" he asked with a rueful look.

"Oh, not too much. Apologies, groveling, long explanations . . . and that was just to explain why I'm friends with you."

With a half grin, Charles shook a knowing finger at Alex. "You would not be joking if she hadn't forgiven you. So everything's settled then between the two of you?"

"Er . . . no." Charles looked slightly concerned, but Alex continued, "Just postponed. Sophia wants to speak to her father before she agrees to anything."

Charles nodded at this news. "It's just a matter of time, then. I have to say, Alex, I'm really pleased for you. And for myself too—you met her at my ball, so you will forever be in my debt now."

"Last time I felt I was in your debt, I stayed here to attend your ball against my better judgment, and look what happened."

"Yes, look what happened. You met a young lady and fell in love. You try to repay me, and you end up more in my debt," Charles said, quite satisfied with himself.

"I didn't fall in love," Alex was quick to deny.

Charles's voice was cajoling. "Come, Alex, you can tell me. No use trying to hide it now. You certainly weren't when she was here."

Alex gave an expressive eye roll at Charles's banter. "It's not love, Charles. In case you've forgotten, she and I have to marry."

Charles turned more serious as he asked, "Do you still see it that way?"

"That's the way it is. Sophia and I will get along fine, but it's certainly not a love match."

Charles's expression showed he didn't believe a word. "I won't deny that the two of you got off to a rocky start. But I think that, despite the way things began, you and Sophia are made for each other."

"No, we're not," Alex denied again. "We're just two people who have been thrown together against our will. Not everyone is as lucky as you and Lucy."

Charles narrowed his eyes, scrutinizing Alex to see if he meant what he said. "You believe that now, but you'll realize I'm right eventually. I'm always right."

Alex glared at Charles' smug expression, but he let the subject drop. In his experience Charles *was* always right.

Twenty-Two

Sophia knew she had put off the visit to her grandmother's solicitor long enough. When she had been staying with Aunt Nora, there had never been an opportunity. She had asked if they could stop by one day, but Aunt Nora wouldn't interrupt their days of socializing with a boring visit like that. And, of course, since meeting Mr. Alexander Huntley, her mind had been excessively occupied with other matters.

Today would be a quiet day at Dalton House; no parties or events were planned until this evening. Sophia decided this might be the most convenient time to run her errand. Alex had called on them more than once for a morning visit, but Sophia felt that she would rather not see him this morning, her thoughts from the night before still troubling her.

"Sir Henry, would it be too much trouble for me to use your carriage this morning?" she asked at breakfast. "I need to meet with my solicitor on Chapel Street."

Both Lord and Lady Fitzgerald looked at Sophia with surprised and puzzled expressions. Sir Henry questioned, "Your solicitor, Miss Spencer?"

"Yes, my solicitor. His name is Mr. Wilson," she said.

"Why do you have a solicitor, and why do you need to meet with him?" asked Sir Henry.

"Oh, I forgot. Since you haven't been in Tissington, you probably haven't heard about my grandmother, Lady Atkinson, leaving me an inheritance. Mr. Wilson is really my grandmother's solicitor. He told me to come to his London office on Chapel Street to sign some documents. I'm not sure what exactly . . ."

Lady Anne was looking at her with avid interest. "Just how much has your grandmother left you, Sophia?"

"Ahh . . . I don't actually know," Sophia admitted sheepishly. "Mr. Wilson described the investments when he told me about my inheritance, but I was too overwhelmed by it all to remember to ask what the investments are worth."

Sophia clearly remembered that day when Mr. Wilson had been waiting for her when she returned from her ride. He had spoken at length about grandmother's investments and the terms of the will, about the bank and his London office, and about signing documents, but Sophia had stopped absorbing new information after Mr. Wilson had told her that she would receive twenty pounds per month. Her thoughts had reeled with the enormity of it all. *Twenty pounds—every month!* That alone was an enormous fortune to her; she could be happy forever with twenty pounds a month. She had daydreamed, as Mr. Wilson talked, about all that she could do with so much money. She could have a new riding habit and a new saddle for Pearl. Her father had wanted to repair the chimneys in the servants' quarters last fall but had put it off. And the carpet in the dining hall that she had spilled on too many times to come clean could finally be replaced. She could do it all in the very first month, and then there would be another twenty pounds coming the next month. And then twenty more the next month. And then twenty more pounds after that! It had been almost incomprehensible.

The reality had been just as good as she had hoped. That twenty pounds each month had been an absolute luxury in the months leading up to her trip to London. But her daydreaming had caused her to miss most of what Mr. Wilson had told her, which was why she was still a bit confused about the inheritance.

She wished she could describe her inheritance to the Fitzgeralds in detail, but the truth was that she just didn't know. Trying to be helpful, Sophia cleared her throat and tried to answer Lady Anne's question by describing what she could remember. "He said something about a granary in the north somewhere, and a shipping line that trades in . . . the Orient, I think. Well, if I can use your carriage this morning, then I'll be sure to ask Mr. Wilson for more detailed information this time."

Lord and Lady Fitzgerald were, as married couples sometimes do, giving each other a significant look that communicated the importance of this new information. Sir Henry proposed a different plan. "Actually, Miss Spencer, my meetings in Parliament won't begin until well into the afternoon today. How about if I accompany you to Chapel Street?"

Sophia was grateful. "Oh, would you? That would be wonderful! Then you can help me understand it all better."

"Of course, Miss Spencer. I am happy to help you in any way I can. I'll send a note to Mr. Wilson that we'll be in to see him this morning. Let's leave within the hour." Sophia smiled and left the breakfast room to get ready.

❦

Lady Anne was very pleased with this development. Sophia had long been a favorite of hers, and having Sophia as their guest had only strengthened that feeling. Her manners were lovely, but more than that, her character was lovely. She never failed to please, and Lady Anne had speculated before how high a connection Sophia could have achieved had she been born with rank. With no money and her father a country doctor, Lady Anne knew that in regards to Sophia's union to Mr. Huntley the advantage was all on Sophia's side. But if Sophia had received even a small sum from her maternal grandmother, it would, perhaps, make her much more the equal of Mr. Huntley. The marriage was inevitable, of course, but a little dowry for the bride could be a great equalizer.

Before leaving with Sir Henry, Lady Anne found the opportunity to ask, "Sophia, does Mr. Huntley know about this inheritance of yours?"

Sophia nodded. "Yes. In fact, I thought that was why I was in this situation in the first place. Aunt Nora told me he was a fortune hunter and wanted my inheritance; she said he must have planned the whole thing." After their evening at the Ashbys', Lady Anne had heard the whole story about Mr. Huntley's past and how he had been labeled a fortune hunter. Sophia went on, "Of course, later I realized that couldn't have been the case because I'm the one who fell asleep in his room." Sophia blushed. Her next words were rushed, as if to cover up her embarrassment. "Then later, of course, he was so angry about the wedding that I knew he couldn't have planned it. And then I thought that perhaps he really is a fortune hunter and wasn't happy being trapped into marrying me when the inheritance probably isn't much to speak of."

Lady Anne thought about that for a moment. "Is this inheritance from your grandmother widely known about, then?"

This time Sophia rolled her eyes. "I'm sure everyone in Tissington knew about it before Mr. Wilson's carriage had reached the edge of the county."

Lady Anne brought the subject back to what she was most

interested in. "I understand that all of Tissington knows about it, but what about here in London? Did your aunt make it known, or did you mention it at all?"

Sophia shrugged. "I don't recall mentioning it to anyone. It seemed impolite to talk about money, but I'm sure my aunt must have told people. At the very least, Mr. Huntley must have heard about it from her when they were arranging all the details for the wedding."

"You weren't there when the arrangements were made?"

Sophia looked sheepish again as she replied, "No, I was asleep when they discussed everything, and my aunt wouldn't wake me."

Lady Anne thought on that for a moment. From her conversations with Mr. Huntley, she was sure he didn't know about it. In fact, she was sure that no one in London knew. A young lady with an inheritance would be talked about.

Lady Anne was now fairly certain that Sophia's aunt had orchestrated the entire scandal surrounding Mr. Huntley and Sophia, and she waned to know why. This newly discovered inheritance made her fairly certain. Lady Bloomfield must have been devastated that her mother didn't leave the fortune to her. And because she couldn't have the money, perhaps she was vindictive enough to want no one to have it—so she made sure that Sophia was found alone with a well-known fortune hunter. A ridiculous scheme, to be sure, but nothing else seemed as likely.

Thinking quickly, Lady Anne advised Sophia, "I think you are right not to mention the money. Yes, I quite agree with you. It would be vulgar to talk about it in polite company."

Sophia nodded her acquiescence, and the subject was dropped. Sir Henry came from his library then, ready to escort Sophia, and they departed. Watching the carriage pull away, Lady Anne felt pleased with herself for thinking so quickly. It was obvious that Mr. Huntley and Sophia were close to reaching an understanding, but the situation was still delicate. If the knowledge of her inheritance came out too soon, his pride or hers could still get in the way. But if it could remain a secret until the engagement was secure, or even until after the wedding, then no doubt they would be happy when the discovery was made.

෴

After a short carriage ride from Dalton House, Sophia and Sir Henry arrived on Chapel Street and were shown in to Mr. Wilson's expensive but simply decorated office.

Sophia wondered what Mr. Wilson's impression of her had been when he came to Tissington.

She remembered what her impression of him had been. She had never met anyone like him before, but she had instantly known that he was a dignified man of business. It had been such a surprise to her that someone so stately and imposing was calling on her that she had frozen in place. She had tried to recover quickly from her shock, but likely he thought she was an inelegant girl without a saving grace.

As Mr. Wilson rose from his desk to greet her and Sir Henry, Sophia realized that he was exactly the same as the last time she'd met him. She could see the respect he had for Sir Henry, and she hoped that his opinion of her would improve—by association at least. Mr. Wilson spoke to her in the exact same way as before, but she thought he was slightly more impressed. It was difficult to tell because Mr. Wilson was eloquent and concise in all his business.

Sir Henry had sent word they were coming, so Mr. Wilson was prepared for their arrival. Sophia forced herself to pay strict attention as he gestured to his large desk on which sat several piles of papers. "Miss Spencer, each of these stacks of documents represents ownership of invested moneys in various schemes. There is a clause at the end of each document stating the transfer of ownership due to the decease of your grandmother. Your signature at this time will make the contract valid, and when you reach the age of twenty-five or marry, all will be available to you to continue or dissolve as you choose."

There were four documents; in addition to the granary were two shipping companies and a large wool farm. Sophia understood the descriptions of her investments better this time. Mr. Wilson explained how her grandmother had been quite savvy with her money and had invested it after carefully considering each venture. "The initial investments totaled a little more than eight thousand pounds," Mr. Wilson explained, "but each of the four investments is profitable, and the money has been earning interest for several years. That, plus an additional fifteen thousand in the funds, are Miss Spencer's primary inheritance."

Sophia's chin dropped. "So more than twenty-three thousand pounds?"

Mr. Wilson merely nodded his head once in confirmation. She looked at Sir Henry, who resembled a statue at the moment. He was probably trying to process the fact that the young lady sitting before him had just made an exorbitant leap upward in the social classes. Even Sophia knew that being in possession of such a sum would make her highly eligible.

Sophia herself was almost as overwhelmed as before. This was the second time she had been told of her inheritance, but its enormity shocked her.

Mr. Wilson didn't wait for them to recover. "As I detailed to you previously, Miss Spencer, the majority of your inheritance will come into your custody when you marry or reach the age of twenty-five. The terms that would make the contract rescindable are matrimony without endorsement of your late grandmother's executor or one appointed by the executor, a permanent removal to a foreign land, or any mismanagement of funds, again to be determined by the executor."

Sophia was about to ask Mr. Wilson to repeat that—something

had caught her attention that she was sure she had missed in Tissington—but before she could, Sir Henry exclaimed, "Wilson, are you saying that Miss Spencer can't marry without some unknown executor's permission? Why, that's preposterous!"

"The executor is not unknown. I have been appointed as executor, as Miss Spencer has been informed," came his calm reply.

"Miss Spencer, were you aware of this?" Sir Henry asked.

Sophia was alarmed. "No, I didn't know!" Then turning to Mr. Wilson, she said, "Sir, you have to believe that I was overwhelmed when you came to see me before, and I'm quite sure that I don't remember these details!"

Sir Henry ran his hands through his hair. The amount of money being discussed made the situation quite serious. "We need to protect the girl's interests, and to do that she needs to *understand* every word. She was almost married with no idea that such a stipulation existed."

Sophia noticed Mr. Wilson's perfect composure break at that news. His eyes rounded in surprise. "But she is not married, correct?"

"No, fortunately not, but not because she had any idea that she couldn't without permission. I've never heard of such a clause. Lady Atkinson couldn't have been quite right in her head, to think she could control Miss Spencer's life and her money from beyond the grave!"

Mr. Wilson went back to his unruffled state as he replied, "Actually these types of stipulations aren't unusual, especially when so much wealth is involved, though I did advise her ladyship against setting up so many restrictions. However, she wasn't satisfied until the will was thus stipulated. She had often expressed disappointment over her three daughters and was adamant that her carefully managed money not be wasted by falling into unworthy hands."

Sir Henry continued to express his disapproval of the whole

thing. But Sophia, who had been thinking about this clause and its effect on her, suddenly asked, "Mr. Wilson, what happens to the money if I don't meet grandmother's requirements?"

Mr. Wilson smiled ruefully. "A lot of work for me, I'm afraid. The contingency is quite extensive and involves dividing the inheritance, but your aunt, Lady Bloomfield would receive the majority."

Sophia sat back, slightly stunned at this. So it *was* her aunt behind everything after all! She had never wanted to believe it, but now there was no doubt. Sophia felt a mix of self-pity and betrayal. Sir Henry, however, seemed more concerned with what was to be done next. "Well then, Mr. Wilson, if you are the executor of this ridiculous will, all of Miss Spencer's suitors will have to be sent to you before she can accept any offers. Is that so?"

"Yes. Any prospective husband of Miss Spencer will need to be approved before the nuptials take place. I will need to verify that his character and financial standing meet with the standard stipulated in the will."

As these words were uttered, Sophia's heart sunk low. All hope for her future seemed finally to be over. Mr. Wilson would never approve of Alexander Huntley as an appropriate husband for Sophia. Alex had told her about the poor state of his finances that his father had left him. And once Mr. Wilson learned that Alex was considered a fortune hunter, the marriage would never be permitted.

For a moment, Sophia thought that she could marry Alex anyway, knowing that the inheritance would be taken away from her. But she quickly realized that it was out of the question. Sophia knew that she couldn't marry Alex without her inheritance. He had referred to taking on a wife as a burden. A wife was just the kind of responsibility he wanted to avoid, but his sense of honor had made him try to win her over. Sophia didn't know if Alex really wanted to marry her, but she acknowledged to herself that she had almost been convinced to marry him. In that moment, she had decided that she would be the least demanding wife ever so that he wouldn't regret it. And, of course, coming into the marriage with an inheritance, even a small one, would have helped her feel that she was contributing. But to marry Alex now would mean giving up the entire fortune her grandmother had left her, and she couldn't marry him with nothing. She wouldn't. He had been through enough.

It was little consolation to realize that by not marrying Alex she would keep her large inheritance. Aunt Nora had been cunning indeed, and she had nearly gotten her hands on a share of it. She had almost forced Sophia to the altar without permission from Mr. Wilson—and to a notorious fortune hunter. Sophia realized that she had been far too trusting of Aunt Nora. Everyone else had suspected that her aunt was behind the scandal, but Sophia had thought they were wrong. She hadn't known how her aunt stood to profit from such a thing, but now it was only too plain to see. Aunt Nora had schemed up this plan and manipulated Sophia.

Sophia's head was beginning to ache. Mr. Wilson and Sir Henry were still talking over the terms of the will. Mr. Wilson was droning on in his official and technical way, but Sophia didn't want to hear it anymore. She wanted to escape from his perfect office. With only that thought in mind, she stood abruptly, interrupting the conversation by begging to take her leave.

Mr. Wilson reminded her that she had not yet signed the documents. She hardly had the patience to put her name to each of the papers. It suddenly seemed to not mean very much at all.

Sir Henry was solicitous and helped Sophia to the carriage, although he surprised her by not getting in too. He instructed her to take the carriage home, saying he would "finish speaking with Wilson and then go from here on to the House of Lords."

Sophia bid him good-bye, and the carriage door was shut. She traveled back to Dalton House in silence as hopelessness settled deep inside her heart.

Twenty-Three

Several hours later, Sophia was preparing for an evening out. She couldn't remember what was on the agenda. Last night, her worry about whether Alex really had feelings for her or if they were contrived had seemed to be the most important question of her life. She longed to know the truth. Now it didn't matter at all. If she married him, the inheritance would be taken away, and then he couldn't possibly like her—or even pretend to.

Sophia had dressed for the evening in a gown that her maid had chosen. Judging by the formalness of the gown, Sophia assumed she would be attending a ball later, but she couldn't bring herself to care. She was sitting at her dressing table, letting her head be pulled gently in different directions as her hair was arranged. She stared vacantly at her reflection, wondering why she was bothering at all.

Her maid paused, her expression alert. Sophia heard some commotion from below. It sounded as though a visitor had arrived.

Alex was supposed to meet them at the ball later, but she wondered if he had come to escort her after all. Despite the fact that Sophia told herself not to, her heartbeat quickened, and she pressed a hand to her stomach and blew out a tense breath.

"Thank you, Marie. It looks fine," Sophia said, referring to her hair. She rose and turned to the door.

Sophia picked up her shawl and strode toward the hall. She was quite nervous to see Alex, knowing that there was no future between them any longer. But Alex didn't know, and Sophia didn't know how she could find the words to tell him.

She stopped at the top of the stairs to gather her gown in one hand and lift it out of the way as she descended, but when she looked up, her eyes were met with a surprise visitor. It was her father! She felt her expression lift, and she practically flew down the stairs to embrace him. The unexpected arrival caused commotion. They both spoke at once, asking questions without listening for the answers. Lady Anne came down, and the commotion continued. Hellos were spoken, and hasty explanations were followed by the same explanations in more detail.

Sophia heard the incredulity in her father's voice as he finally told how he came to arrive in London. "After receiving your letter about the trouble you were in—scandalous event, running away from your own wedding, and stating that you wanted to return home—I decided to come to London and bring you back myself."

Sophia threw her arms around her father in a grateful embrace. This was what she had wanted and needed all along. After all her misadventures without him, she knew she had the best father in the world.

Lady Anne led them to the drawing room and left them to their reunion while she finished preparing for the evening out. With her father's arm around her, Sophia started to explain what had happened since she ran away from the wedding.

"Yes, yes," her father interrupted, "you told me about leaving your own wedding before it could take place and your arrival at Dalton House in your letter. But how did you come to be married—or almost married, rather? What happened?"

"Well, it happened as I told you in my other letters, Father . . . I fell asleep at a ball, and it turned out to be Mr. Huntley's room I was sleeping in, and he and I were discovered together before I woke up."

Sophia could see her father's shock and anger. He was obviously hearing this news for the first time. It was a few moments before he could speak. Sophia was surprised; she'd expected him to have a firm understanding of the events.

"Are you telling me that your aunt allowed you to be alone—asleep even—in a gentleman's private room?!" His face was growing red, and Sophia could tell he was trying hard not to raise his voice. "You did not tell me *that* in any of your letters!"

Sophia's father rarely lost his temper; seeing him this way frightened her just a bit. She also felt that any anger toward her was unjustified and quickly became defensive. "Yes, Father, I did tell you all about it! How could you not pay attention? Did you skim over my letters, thinking there would be nothing but frivolous nonsense in them?"

"Of course I read your letters—*every* word of *every* letter," he emphasized. "But a fortnight ago, they suddenly stopped coming. For over a week I heard nothing. Then the next news you send me is that you were supposed to be married but had run away to Lord and Lady Fitzgerald instead. I decided I'd better come and get you straight away, and so I left early the next morning."

Sophia was gently shaking her head in disgusted disbelief. Her aunt had hurt her again. Sophia had written to her father everything that had happened at the ball and leading up to the wedding—long detailed letters, including her growing distaste for Aunt Nora. She hadn't suspected then that her aunt was plotting to get Grandmother Atkinson's money. Finding out that, along with all her other scheming, Aunt Nora had also stolen Sophia's letters to her father was the last straw. Sophia stood up and started pacing, but she wasted no time in telling her father who was to blame for her predicament.

Her explanation was, of necessity, a lengthy one. She had to explain all about grandmother's will and what Mr. Wilson had revealed. Once her father understood Aunt Nora's motivation, it was easier to explain what had happened: how Aunt Nora had made sure Sophia was found with Mr. Huntley and why their marriage would have benefited Aunt Nora. Sophia didn't want to give her father a bad impression of Alex, but she had to explain about his past, how it was well known that his father had lost everything, and that he had left London after a scandalous attempt to elope with a young lady of great fortune. That was why, if she married him, she would lose her inheritance.

A quarter of an hour later, all the relevant details were relayed and understood. Mr. Spencer had exclaimed, "How could this have happened?" at least five times and was just sending Aunt Nora to the devil again when Lady Anne came back in the room.

Lady Anne could see how relieved Sophia was to have her father with her. She, on the other hand, was less pleased to see Mr. Spencer. It wasn't that she didn't like her neighbor and friend from home, but his arrival was disrupting her plans. If he took Sophia away, she and Mr. Huntley would never have a chance to declare their love, and Lady Anne was certain they were close. It was frustrating to say the least.

She hadn't seen her husband since that morning when he had taken Sophia to her solicitor's, so she hadn't had a chance to ask him what he had found out. Sophia had complained of a headache upon her return, and Lady Anne had encouraged her to spend the afternoon resting in her room so she would feel better in time for this evening's ball. Consequently, Lady Anne's curiosity was still unsatisfied. But truly the amount of the inheritance was unimportant; she was simply pleased that Sophia had an inheritance at all, and she was eager to see how the events would unfold.

With these thoughts in mind, Lady Anne said, "Mr. Spencer, I hope you aren't planning on returning to Tissington right away. Sir Henry and I will enjoy having you as our guest during your stay in London. After such a long journey, you'll want to delay your return for a week at least, I'm sure."

Lady Anne was as confident as her words that he would agree, so she was more than disappointed when he responded, "I do appreciate your generosity, Lady Anne, for myself and for having Sophia as well. However, we will only impose on you for one more night. My plan is to leave tomorrow."

"That won't do at all!" she exclaimed. "We have accepted so many invitations that include Sophia. It would be incredibly impolite to cancel now. Couldn't you delay your return for just a few days?" Lady Anne was a bit frustrated with Mr. Spencer's stubbornness, but she should have known better than to appeal to him in that way. She knew he had always cared little about pleasing society, and a few canceled engagements wouldn't matter to him at all.

"I'm sure you can manage fine without Sophia, Lady Anne. Send her apologies and tell your hostesses that it is all my doing. I take all the blame, and you can all abuse me to your hearts' content for taking Sophia away." It was obvious the idea of it diverted him, but Lady Anne was not amused.

"There isn't time to cancel for this evening. Sophia will have to come to the ball tonight at the very least. And perhaps when you see how happy your daughter is here in London with us, you'll decide to stay a bit longer after all."

"Perhaps you are right," he replied without any conviction in his voice. "We'll attend the ball this evening. Thank you, Lady Anne."

Lady Anne could tell she was being placated, but at least he'd agreed to her last plan. Suddenly, everything hinged on the events of this one evening, and Lady Anne found herself doubting for the first time that a happy ending was in store for Mr. Huntley and Sophia. She knew that they had fallen in love over the last week and a half, but she wasn't sure if either of them knew it themselves yet.

Twenty-Four

*A*lex was running late. He had been distracted with thoughts about the future of Boxwell Court now that he would be bringing Sophia there as his bride. Luckily, Boxwell Court itself was out of danger, but if he could convince her to be patient for a few more years, then they could have a family home to be truly proud of. The thought that had actually distracted him—and the cause of his tardiness—was that he remembered a few key assets his father's accountant had overlooked, and he was considering doing a little more business in London before leaving to begin his life with Sophia. Perhaps they wouldn't have to be quite so patient after all. With Sophia at his side, he would finally have it all. In fact, when Charles had suggested a party, he had shot the idea down. But if Sophia wanted to celebrate their marriage with a party at Boxwell Court, then they would have one.

Tonight there was a come-out ball for Lucy's cousin. Alex was eager for this evening because it would be the first time that he and Sophia would dance together. He planned to stand up with her three times. As far as the public knew, they were engaged, so it would be acceptable. He would make sure that one of the three dances was the supper dance so that he could escort her in and monopolize even more of her time. He wanted to spend time with her because he still needed to convince her to marry him, and because he was sure he would still feel uncomfortable being at a ball; it was certainly not because he was in love with her.

Charles had said that he thought Alex was in love with Sophia, but Charles was wrong. She was a beautiful young woman, and Alex admitted that he enjoyed her company, and he felt that if he could undo that awful scene from the last ball, then perhaps he would come to love her.

After being announced in the hall, he said a quick hello to Charles and Lucy, who were necessarily with Lucy's family this evening—it was her cousin's ball, after all. Because he had been distracted, Alex was arriving after the rest of their party, and he knew that Sophia would already be inside with the Fitzgeralds. He made his way directly to the ballroom and looked around for Sir Henry's tall form, but he didn't spot him right away. He began working his way around the side of the ballroom. The dancers were moving uniformly in the center. Alex moved in between those who watched, edging his way around the room. All the while he kept looking for the Fitzgeralds and especially Sophia.

He heard her laugh. Glancing up at the dancers for the first time, he saw her. But the sight awaiting him was most unwelcome. Sophia was promenading through the dance with another man's arm around her, her hand clasped in his. The instant jealousy he felt was a new feeling for Alex, and he was almost overwhelmed by it. He began, on instinct, walking toward the pair with the intention of pulling Sophia out of the man's arms. Luckily, a pair of dancers moved in his way, and he had to step back instead. It gave him a moment to clear his head and realize that Sophia would, naturally, be asked to dance by other men. He had no intention of asking anyone else to dance this evening, so it hadn't occurred to him that Sophia might be asked to dance by someone else. *It doesn't mean anything*, he tried to convince himself, but his enthusiasm for the evening was gone for the moment.

Jealousy was a strange reaction for him to have. Despite what Charles had said, he knew he didn't love Sophia. He liked her, of course, but he wouldn't have predicted he would feel angry just from seeing her dance with another man. He supposed it was more of a protective feeling than jealousy, which made much more sense.

Alex stayed back among those who watched the dance's progression. His eyes followed her, and he noticed how particularly elegant she looked. Her beauty left him breathless. Sophia and her partner were waiting for their turn to promenade when she looked up directly into Alex's unwavering gaze. She didn't smile and neither did he, but their eyes stayed locked on each other for those few seconds. For a moment, he thought she looked almost guilty—perhaps for dancing with another man—but it was fleeting, and the look that she held him captive with was warm. The moment felt significant, but it was over quickly. Sophia's partner reclaimed her attention in time for the pair to promenade to the other side of the room.

It wasn't easy to patiently wait for his turn with her, but he continued to track her from across the room and let himself enjoy the beautiful sight. His anticipation for the evening began to come back, knowing the most beautiful girl at the ball would be his.

Alex was gratified that as soon as the dance ended, Sophia spoke a few words of farewell to her partner and then made her way directly to him.

❧

With the final notes of music in her ears, Sophia said to her father, "I'm impressed that you haven't forgotten how to dance after all these years, Father."

Mr. Spencer rolled his eyes as he always did when Sophia teased him about being too old. He said, "Perhaps your age is catching up to you, my dear. I thought for a moment *you* had forgotten the steps."

Sophia smiled tightly at her father and turned away self-consciously, knowing that for a moment she had forgotten the dance. She had forgotten everything else as well when she'd caught sight of Alex. It was ridiculous that she should feel this way when she had told herself not to, but she felt an all-too-familiar fluttering inside her even now as she was about to go find him. "Yes, perhaps," she agreed with her father distractedly. "I think the Fitzgeralds are in the card room. I'll come and find you there in a bit." And without waiting for his reply, Sophia walked in the direction she had last seen Alex. She found him in the same spot where he had been watching her while she had danced with her father.

He looked pleased to see her, and Sophia felt that he must genuinely like her, at least a little. His plan had been uncovered; there was no reason to pretend for her sake anymore.

He didn't speak at first, and Sophia didn't either; she didn't know what to say. She just took her place next to him and turned to face the room at his side.

Keeping his gaze forward, he leaned toward her and said, "You dance so well. I hope you'll favor me with the next set."

She loved that he spoke to her as though they had only been apart a minute rather than a day. But what a difference this one day had made! Who knew what could have happened if she had never been to Mr. Wilson's office today? But she had gone, and she knew that this was good-bye. Sophia had been looking forward to the ball, knowing she would have the opportunity to dance with Alex, but now she regretted that she had come. This was just prolonging the inevitable and making her wish everything didn't have to end.

When she didn't answer right away, Alex turned to look at her expectantly. Sophia was already feeling incredibly sad at the thought of this being their last time together. She saw Alex's look turn into puzzlement and realized she needed to do better at hiding her devastation.

"Of course, Alex. I would love to dance with you." The words sounded off, but Alex smiled in response and offered her his arm. She resolved then to enjoy this evening as much as she could. All they would have was this one ball together, and she didn't want to ruin it. She put her arm through his, and he led her to the dance floor to join the other couples there. They took their places in the lines and stood facing one another. Alex was staring intently at her. She tried a cheerful smile, but she wasn't sure it was convincing. Trying to avoid his scrutiny, she broke their gaze and looked at the musicians to see if the dance was about to begin.

After a moment the musicians struck up their instruments, and Sophia returned her attention to Alex as they stepped together, joined hands, and turned in a circle. He took the opportunity to ask, "Are you well?"

"Yes" was all she had time to reply before they stepped back again.

Again they came together, and Alex spoke quickly. "The man you were dancing with when I arrived—did he upset you somehow?"

They stepped back again before she could answer. But it wasn't her father who had upset her; it was having to say good-bye to Alex that had left her feeling miserable, but she couldn't explain that as they danced. They waited for a pair of dancers to chassé between them. The dance brought them back together, and Sophia had the chance to lie. "I'm not upset." She attempted a smile to prove it, and her eyes widened with what she hoped was innocence.

Before Alex released her hand, he leaned a little closer and said intimately, "I can't look away. Your smile captivates me."

Sophia was startled enough to miss a step, but quickly regained her footing and stepped back in the line. She had not expected this. Alex was still trying to win her regard. His flattering comment had disarmed her. She was convinced that Alex had been pretending to enjoy her company all along. But now, with no engagement, fake or otherwise, there was no reason for him to compliment her unless he really meant it. She was surprised and, quite truthfully, dismayed.

She admitted to herself that she cared for him. If he courted her in earnest, she would fall completely in love. And it would be a fall that would be impossible to recover from. She shouldn't have come tonight. It was a mistake to think she could be with Alex and only take away memories. She would surely leave with a broken heart as well.

Alex continued to look at her intently as they came together, turned, and moved back again, this time without speaking. She knew she was far more captivated by him than he was by her. She was desperate to break the connection so she glanced quickly around before the dance brought them close together again. She noticed Lady Barrett, Aunt Nora's friend, watching them. For a change of subject, that would have to do.

Sophia placed her hand in Alex's and said as they turned, "Lady Barrett is watching us. Do you think we are still the subject of gossip?"

Alex looked away from Sophia toward Lady Barrett, who was not far from the dancers. There was no doubt from his expression that he recognized her as one of the women who had found them together in his room at the last ball. He didn't look pleased at the reminder and quickly brought his attention back to the dance, as if to ignore such a nuisance. At the next opportunity, Alex said, "Surely we're not interesting to her anymore. She's most likely here looking for the next scandal."

Sophia couldn't help but worry that that was true. Lady Barrett seemed to thrive on scandal. Sophia had met the woman several times in the company of Aunt Nora, but never had Lady Barrett been so animated as on the night of the Evertons' ball when Sophia had made her shameful exit. Lady Barrett was watching them far too closely for Sophia's comfort.

She also noticed Mrs. Sutter in the crowd. Lady Anne's friend had been unable to convince Sophia to have a ball of her own, and she wondered if the older woman resented her for it. Much to Sophia's dismay she had also seen the Brights here this evening. This was the ball she had meant to avoid so that she wouldn't have to see those who had so blatantly snubbed her. And although she hadn't seen Lord and Lady Ashby yet, she had heard someone mention that they would be attending this evening. Sophia felt the pressure of having so many adversaries around her. It would take constant attentiveness to avoid all of them this evening. But at least they would serve as a distraction. There would be no more opportunities for flirting with so much opposition to avoid. These thoughts were almost comforting, and Sophia kept her and Alex's choppy conversation on trivial matters as they finished their set.

Just before the dance ended, Alex saw someone else watching them. It was the gentleman Sophia had been dancing with when he arrived. This was all the reminder he needed that he didn't want anyone else asking Sophia to dance, and so, as he led her off the dance floor, he suggested, "Let's step out to the garden for fresh air." Sophia glanced to where Lady Barrett was standing, but the woman wasn't watching them now. Sophia turned back to him and nodded.

They stopped just outside the door, where there was still plenty of light spilling out. Alex wanted to re-create the close connection he had felt with her during the dance, and he was trying to think of a way to do that when Sophia's dance partner stepped outside too. Alex was beginning to be quite annoyed with the man's persistence.

He was about to suggest that they venture farther out into the garden when the other man said, "Sophia, you shouldn't be out here without a chaperone."

"Your concern is unnecessary, sir," Alex answered for her. "Miss Spencer and I are engaged."

"No, you are not engaged," the man contradicted him with confidence.

Alex couldn't believe the audacity of this gentleman. Although it was true that they weren't actually engaged to be married, as far as the world was concerned they were. He reached down and clasped Sophia's hand. The gesture felt so right and comfortable, yet at the same time he felt his heart race from the physical contact. He had to clear his throat and focus on the gentleman standing in front of him once more before responding.

"Yes, we are. Miss Spencer and I have an understanding." To make it even more convincing, he turned to look into her eyes as he said, "Don't we, Sophia?"

His first clue that Sophia wasn't about to support him in the lie was the cringe in her expression. She bit the side of her bottom lip as she stared back at Alex with regret.

Alex was momentarily distracted. The gentleman took another step toward them and cleared his throat, which snapped Alex back to the moment.

"Alex, I'd like to introduce you to my father, Mr. William Spencer," Sophia finally said, pushing the words out of her mouth. "Father, this is Mr. Alexander Huntley, whom I've been telling you about."

Alex felt foolish but relieved. The man was her father. If he had actually looked at the gentleman, he probably would have realized that he was too old for Sophia and seen there was even a bit of family resemblance. But his envy had clouded any rational thought. He had certainly just given his future father-in-law a terrible first impression.

An awkward pause followed Sophia's introduction, and Alex was the one cringing now. He reached out his hand and was relieved that Mr. Spencer took it. With a handshake they became acquainted, but Alex knew he would have to fix matters. "I apologize, Mr. Spencer, for contradicting you before. Of course your daughter and I don't have an understanding at present, but we have been trying to diffuse the scandal by telling everyone that we are engaged."

Mr. Spencer didn't look exactly pleased to be meeting him, and he looked less than convinced by the apology Alex had offered. Alex recalled that Sophia had introduced him as the man she had been telling her father about, and he suddenly wondered if he had made a poor impression with her father before they even met. Actually, just the basic facts of their situation would cause any parent displeasure. Mr. Spencer still hadn't replied, and Alex could almost feel his disapproval. *Time to change that*, he thought.

"It's wonderful that you've come. I was going to travel to Tissington to see you."

"Were you?" came his clipped reply.

"Ah . . . yes? Er, yes, I was. I meant to ask your permission to marry your daughter."

"You didn't seem to need it the first time around."

Alex hadn't been expecting an interrogation this evening, and the stern look he was receiving from Mr. Spencer was causing his collar to feel tight. The next set was about to begin; he could hear the musicians starting up.

"Lady Bloomfield was very insistent that the wedding take place as soon as possible," Alex said. But he could see immediately that deflecting the blame was not improving Mr. Spencer's demeanor. "But I shouldn't have been influenced by her, and I apologize for not delaying the wedding until you were consulted." Truthfully, it hadn't even crossed his mind before the wedding. He had assumed that Sophia's father must not play a significant role in her life because he had only seen her with her aunt.

Sophia jumped to his defense at this point. "Father, you can't fault Alex with that. I told you how my aunt planned it all."

Alex was grateful that Sophia seemed to be on his side. He tried to covertly smile at her, but she looked away without returning the gesture. He didn't have time to wonder about that, however, because Mr. Spencer addressed him again. "So you wanted to ask my permission to marry my daughter . . . what will you do if I say no?"

Alex pulled back in surprise at this question. Perhaps Sophia hadn't explained the whole situation to him—no father would say no to a marriage that would save his daughter's reputation. Alex knew, ever since he had read her note after she left the wedding, that Sophia thought she had a choice about whether or not they married, but surely her father knew better.

Alex glanced at Sophia, whose head was turned away as though she disliked the subject. Turning again to Mr. Spencer, he asked, "Did Sophia explain the situation, sir?" Instinctively, Alex lowered his voice as he related the embarrassing details. "We were discovered together in my room by several matrons who are known for gossip. Our supposed engagement has barely staved off society's rejection, and our marriage will be the only thing to restore our honor. With your permission, Mr. Spencer, I think we should be married as soon as possible." It felt strange to be having this conversation right outside a crowded ballroom with everyone inside carrying on dancing. Laughter floated out, but it didn't change the tense atmosphere as Alex waited for Mr. Spencer's reply.

Finally, Sophia's father gave Alex a shrewd look. "Very well, Mr. Huntley. You have my permission to marry my daughter." Alex was on the point of breathing a sigh of relief when Mr. Spencer continued, "But as to when—or, rather, *if*—you marry her, well, that is entirely up to her."

Alex couldn't believe what he had just heard. "You cannot—" he spluttered.

But Mr. Spencer interrupted him. "Sophia is my daughter, and in whatever she chooses she will have my support. Society may reject her as you say, but Tissington is far from London and its rules. I will not allow anyone to hurt her, and if she chooses not to marry you, then you will have to accept that."

Alex stared at Mr. Spencer incredulously. All he got in return was a challenging look, and Alex realized that he was waiting for him to ask Sophia right then.

It was unbelievable to him how this conversation was going. He knew she didn't love him yet, but he had been thinking that he still had plenty of time to convince her that she cared for him, enough to justify marriage. Now it was all to be decided in a moment. And looking at Sophia, he could already see a look of regret in her eyes.

"Sophia, please . . ." He didn't even know what he was about to ask, but he could see she was going to say no and he felt helpless, as though everything was spinning out of his control. He hadn't felt this way since the night he had discovered her sleeping in his room; it was as though someone had pulled the rug out from under his feet.

When he just stood there with his question unasked, Sophia finally took pity on him and turned to her father. "Father, may I speak with Mr. Huntley privately for a moment?" she asked.

Alex's hopes continued to plummet. She was back to calling him Mr. Huntley again. And surely, if she was going to say yes, she would have asked for more than a moment of private conversation.

"Of course, Sophia. I'll be with Sir Henry and Lady Anne," he replied. With one last challenging look at Alex, he turned toward the door and went back inside.

Sophia didn't speak right away, but her expression was sorrowful. Alex had a mad urge to start begging before she could say the words that would send him away. But he quelled the desire as he saw her resolved expression.

"I'm so sorry that I ever got us into this situation. I realize now that it really was my fault." Alex tried to interrupt, but Sophia waved a hand to stop him. "I know, I know. My aunt planned it all. But I was so naïve and trusting—" She closed her eyes and shook her head. "I'm just grateful that I can release you now from your obligation toward me. As you can see, my father will protect me from the consequences. So you don't have to marry me."

"Sophia, this is a mistake." She just shook her head without looking up, and Alex could see that she was determined. He tried to keep the desperation out of his voice as he said, "You must realize that for your honor and for mine, we have to marry. We can't walk away from this. You and I will both suffer if you don't agree to marry me." It was silent for several long moments as Alex searched for any words that would convince her. Finally, he just simply said, "Besides, it's what I want." Alex took a fortifying breath. "Will you marry me?"

To his surprise, Sophia didn't say no. She closed her eyes again, and there was a serene look on her face. Alex hardly dared allow himself to hope, but in that moment he thought he might have a chance. Then Sophia opened her eyes, and he saw the same sad regretful look. He felt his pride come to his rescue as she looked at him that way. She wasn't going to change her mind, and he wasn't going to be pitied.

❧

For that one brief blissful moment, Sophia let herself believe that Alex meant it—that he wanted to marry her. But she knew it wasn't true. Even if her foolish heart wanted to believe it, her mind knew better. All along, Alex had insisted on saving her reputation. She had known before she spoke that he would try to change her mind. But her mind couldn't be changed. And besides, when Alex found out that she would lose her inheritance if she married him, he would never want her. He would act like he did and still try to convince her they should marry; he was too honorable and self-sacrificing to let her go too easily.

Sophia was sure that Alex thought they would suffer if they didn't marry, but Sophia knew they would suffer much more if they did. Her regretful look stopped Alex from speaking. He had looked, just a moment before, like he was going to say more, but he didn't. He took a step back and crossed his arms.

He looked splendid this evening; no other man compared to him in the least. He looked so tall and handsome in his dark blue coat. As she had danced with him, she couldn't help but notice that his blue eyes seemed a darker shade this evening as well. But more than his striking looks, she loved how even after all he had been through, he still carried himself with confidence. He looked so strong—like he could support her through anything. But a marriage between them now would make him hate her. It would be unbearable.

Sophia again wished he were hers. How contrary was her nature that she only wanted something—or someone, rather—when she could no longer have him.

Finally, Sophia said, "What a strange acquaintance we've had." She tried to speak with finality, making it obvious that their strange acquaintance was at an end. She paused for a moment to give herself the courage to say what she had to say. "The entire time I've known you, marriage has been hanging over us like an executioner's sword. I know you thought we didn't have a choice, but we do. No one is forcing us anymore. We can choose what we want." Sophia looked at Alex closely as she said this, but his look was impossible to read, his emotions closed off. She let the pause lengthen, hoping he'd say something. He briefly nodded to acknowledge her words, but he wasn't about to speak.

"We aren't in love, of course, so there is no reason for us to choose to marry." She looked for any sign of a difference of opinion from him. He seemed to assess her for several long seconds. Sophia tried to keep her emotions hidden; she wasn't sure she succeeded. She wanted so badly for him to contradict her. It wouldn't solve anything, of course; she still couldn't marry him even if he did love her. But she would rather have a tragic love story than no love story at all.

Alex merely echoed her words: "We aren't in love . . . of course."

The silence lengthened, and Sophia knew she couldn't hold back her tears for long. She needed to leave before Alex saw how much this was hurting her. She had to swallow the lump in her throat twice before she could speak. "My father and I will be returning to Tissington first thing in the morning, so I won't be seeing you again." She stopped to take a calming breath. "Good-bye, Alex." It sounded dismissive and rude, but Sophia couldn't have said it any other way without losing her careful control.

Alex looked at her for a moment longer, perhaps to see if she really meant it. And then, obviously believing that their good-bye meant nothing to her, he replied, "Good-bye, Miss Spencer." Then he turned and walked back inside.

Sophia followed him with her gaze until he was lost in the crowd and her eyes were blurry with tears. Her father must have been watching the door, because he soon stepped out to find her. She had moved a few steps farther from the window, so hopefully the dim light wouldn't reveal the wetness in her eyes. She tried to discreetly wipe them before her father reached her.

He didn't have to ask what her decision was. Alex leaving alone made it quite clear. She put her arm through her father's and asked, "Can we leave now?" He nodded in the affirmative.

Twenty-Five

*A*lex left the ball, eager to put as much distance as possible between himself and the scene behind him. He couldn't believe this was happening to him again. The circumstances were different from the last time, but the result was the same; he was leaving London in humiliation and without the wife he thought he'd had. The unfairness of it all made him angry. How many times would he have to face unfair and humiliating circumstances in his life?

The humiliation he could handle; he'd handled it before. With enough pride to rival any in England, he wouldn't let anyone see how much he was suffering. And the feeling of anger washing over him almost felt good in a strange way, giving him a restless energy. His mood was black, but at least it wasn't bleak. He had a deep feeling of dread when he thought about what was waiting for him after the humiliation and the anger receded.

He couldn't stand the thought of seeing anyone, so arriving

back at Charles and Lucy's, he went directly to his rooms and began packing. He was determined to be on the road at first light.

Unfortunately, it took very little time for him to pack his things, and soon the job was done. With nothing to do but pace the floor, the sadness that he had been holding at bay became almost overwhelming.

Sophia didn't love him.

She knew him now—really knew his character and the sort of man he was. And she didn't want him. She still preferred a ruined reputation to a life spent at his side. Her rejection made him feel worthless and more alone than he had ever been. He wished he could leave right then, but it was a moonless night, and he would have to wait until dawn. The only comfort he could look forward to was the all-too familiar isolation of Boxwell Court. Even that left him feeling depressed. What was the point of restoring Boxwell Court to its former glory if he didn't have Sophia to share it with?

The only possible reason that he could need her so badly was that he loved her. He loved her, but she didn't love him. Charles had been right about his feelings after all; Alex just hadn't realized it at the time. Why did Charles always have to be right? He would have felt much better if he had never loved her, or at least had never realized that what he felt was love. But there was nothing he could do about it now. Sophia had been clear: she didn't love him so she wouldn't marry him.

Alex felt as though his energy had been sapped from him, and he slumped down into a chair. His mind was restless, and he wanted to pace, but he felt as though invisible hands were holding him down, and he couldn't find the strength to overcome.

It was less than an hour later when Charles and Lucy returned. He didn't want to see them and wished he was asleep, but it was far too early for that. Charles must have dragged Lucy away from her cousin's ball early once they'd noticed that Alex had left. With a momentous effort, Alex rose from his seat and went downstairs to meet them, knowing it would not be an easy conversation.

He entered the drawing room with a lack of enthusiasm that must have been alarming because Charles asked, "Alex, what has happened? Are you unwell?" Alex just shook his head, but his despondency caused Charles and Lucy to exchange alarmed looks.

"Has something happened to Sophia?" Lucy asked.

Alex shook his head again, and rather than make his friends guess further, he gave a brief explanation. "Sophia's father arrived in London today," he said with little emotion in his voice. "He's taking her home tomorrow." He paused so he could say the next part without his voice breaking. "She's refused my offer of marriage. Her father supports her decision."

Charles pulled back in surprise at this announcement. "That's not possible. Surely her father didn't understand the situation or he would have never agreed." He spoke with such conviction. But he hadn't heard the conversation; he didn't know how it was.

"Sophia told her father everything, and he said he would support her decision." Alex stated unequivocally.

"Alex, you have to go back and explain it all yourself. Sophia never thought the situation was serious enough for all the fuss that came from it. You told me what she said right before the wedding, how she had exclaimed over having to get married just because she fell asleep at a ball. To her, it was almost inconsequential, and that's how she must have portrayed it for her father. That's the only way he could think that she could decide not to marry you."

Charles's words should have given Alex hope, but they didn't. Not at all. In fact, they just served to remind him that the only way Sophia would ever be his was if she were forced. Swallowing his pride, he finally admitted, "Charles, even if her father changed his mind, Sophia doesn't want to marry me. I asked. She said no."

Charles looked almost as sad as Alex felt. Alex appreciated the sympathy of his friend, but he again wished for solitude.

"There has to be a reason," Lucy said. Alex had forgotten that Lucy was in the room because she had been so quiet.

"What do you mean?" asked Charles.

But Lucy looked at Alex as she explained, "When we all dined here together, Sophia seemed captivated by you. Even after Charles gave it away that the engagement was real, she still blushed when she caught your gaze." Lucy shook her head as she tried to puzzle it out. "Something must have changed, Alex. There has to be a reason she said no."

Alex replied bitterly, "The only thing that changed was her father arriving and giving her an escape. She never wanted to marry me." Alex could see that Charles and Lucy were going to argue further, but his grief was making him too tired for arguing. "Let's just forget it, please." He started to leave, but then he turned back to say, "I'm leaving in the morning. I'll see you at breakfast, and then be on my way." He had actually been planning to leave before breakfast, but he owed so much to his friends that he decided to at least say good-bye before leaving.

Back in his room, Alex sat on the same sofa he had found Sophia sleeping on weeks ago. He ran his hand gently over the fabric, then rolled his eyes at his sentimentality. He definitely needed to leave. At Boxwell Court there would be no reminders of Sophia Spencer to make him act like a fool over his unrequited love.

Twenty-Six

The next morning, Alex ate an early breakfast with Charles and Lucy. He had two long days of driving ahead of him. But during his restless night, he had decided that he would take care of one last business item before leaving London.

About a year after his father's death, Alex had been sorting through his grandfather's books. If his father had thought there was anything of value in any of them, he would have gambled it away ages ago. Luckily, it was Alex who came across the document folded into the pages of an old French novel. It was a strong-box deposit notice with an inventory of several family heirlooms. There were listed several small but valuable items that had been given to his ancestors by Prince Rupert and Charles II, as well as several larger items that had been collected by his grandfather in foreign lands.

If Alex had found that document within the first few months after his father's death, he would have rushed up to London and sold them the first chance he got. Fortunately, however, he had already begun to turn things around. He remembered feeling positive about the future and decided he would only sell the family heirlooms as a last resort. If things took a turn for the worse—for example, if any of the crops were ruined—then at least he could buy himself more time. But very quickly Alex came to see those heirlooms as a symbol for his success. Only when they were safe from ever having to be sold would he feel that he had truly saved Boxwell Court.

Last night, before arriving at the ball, he had considered selling them anyway. They were far less important to him than Sophia, and selling them would have put Boxwell Court completely out of debt, and they could have begun their marriage by looking toward the future instead of working to undo past mistakes. But now Alex wanted to retrieve his family heirlooms and return them to Boxwell Court because accomplishing this last task would mean he wouldn't have any reason to come to London again for a very long time.

He was immensely disappointed that he wasn't bringing a bride home to Boxwell Court. At least he would be returning with the family heirlooms. But try as he may, he just couldn't bring himself to feel the triumph that he had expected to feel on this occasion.

After Alex explained his errand, Charles decided to accompany him to Threadneedle Street and say his good-bye from there. So Alex bid a sad farewell to Lucy and set off with Charles for the bank.

During the short ride, Charles tried again to persuade Alex to talk to Sophia once more, but it was too painful of a subject for Alex.

"It would be no use. Besides, she's left London by now," Alex told Charles. The carriage ride was silent after that, both friends left somber by the conclusion.

After stepping down from the carriage, they were walking toward the bank when Alex caught the eye of someone familiar. He took a few more steps before familiarity was replaced by recognition, and he turned to glare at Lady Nora Bloomfield.

Apparently she had visited Sophia only once during her stay with the Fitzgeralds. Since then, he hadn't seen or heard of her. But she didn't look reticent as she marched up to Alex. "Is it true? Is the wedding really off?"

This was the last thing Alex needed. His friends' sympathy was difficult enough to bear; he didn't want to also deal with the animosity of this woman who had tried to ruin his life. *Little does she know that she succeeded in ruining his life*, he considered ruefully *just not in the way she had intended.*

Alex tried to keep outwardly calm as he requested, "Lady Bloomfield, please step aside."

But she wasn't about to leave. "Lady Barrett was at the ball last evening. She has informed me that my niece left with her father. Apparently everyone soon heard that my worthless brother-in-law had come to London to take Miss Spencer home—*unmarried!*"

Neither Alex nor Charles, who was now by his side, said a word. They just glared down at Lady Bloomfield until she asked again through gritted teeth, "Is it true that the scandal continues?"

Alex was annoyed that he and Sophia were the subject of gossip again. But he couldn't fight that; he was helpless against gossip. He was relieved to know that Sophia had left London that morning and was safe from it. He, too, would soon be out of the range where gossip could affect him. "Yes, it's true. She has left London, and there will be no wedding."

To Alex's greatest astonishment, Lady Bloomfield's gloved hand met his cheek with some force. The unexpected strike almost knocked him off balance. "You've ruined my life!" she screeched at him. "I'll never get the money now. Everything was going to work.

It almost worked. It's your fault! It is because of you that I have to live like a pauper in the country."

Charles and Alex were both staring at Lady Bloomfield, who seemed to have gone mad before their very eyes. She lunged again at Alex, but this time she only managed to push her hands in his face briefly before he distanced himself from her. Charles stepped around her and pinned her arms to her side.

Lady Bloomfield tried to jerk out of Charles's grasp. When that didn't work, she seemed to finally recall her dignity and demanded, "Release me at once!"

Tentatively, Charles pulled away, ready to restrain the woman again if necessary. Alex cautiously watched for her next move.

She looked like she was contemplating violence again. She leaned toward Alex, who leaned away from her in response. Her eyes darted to Charles and back to Alex again. Realizing she was helpless, she let out a muted but frustrated scream. "I can't believe I let my mother dictate my life," she muttered to herself, "and this is how she repays me." She continued to mumble as she walked away, ignoring Alex and Charles. "And now Sophia gets all my money . . ."

There was a beat of silence between Charles and Alex as they watched her depart. Then Charles clapped Alex on the back and said, "I think she's enamored with you."

Alex was far too surprised at what had just happened to appreciate Charles's humor, but he managed to reply blandly, "Well, my charm is irresistible."

"Another conquest, my friend." But the tension quickly returned. "Do you have any idea what she was talking about?" Charles asked.

"None whatsoever. And that bit at the end . . . she said something about . . ." He cleared his throat to force her name out. "About Sophia. I don't think I can leave London without knowing what she meant."

"Why didn't you say so? Let's go after her and make her explain herself!" cried Charles.

Alex put a hand on his arm to stop him. "How about if we ask the Fitzgeralds first? They might know what Lady Bloomfield was enraged about. Besides, Lady Anne is far less enamored with me than Lady Bloomfield, and will therefore be less likely to fling herself at my head."

As they began walking back to the carriage, Alex added, "If the Fitzgeralds don't have any information, then we'll call on Lady Bloomfield and insist she explain herself."

Alex hoped they wouldn't have to take that step; he'd rather not run into Lady Bloomfield again anytime soon—or ever, for that matter.

Twenty-Seven

When the carriage arrived at Dalton House, Charles and Alex were led directly to the drawing room. Alex had called on the Fitzgeralds enough times recently to be well known to the servants. He and Charles waited several minutes for Lady Anne to appear.

When she did finally arrive, she seemed distracted. *Distracted and maybe nervous*, Alex thought. Her nervousness was uncharacteristic; Alex had only ever seen her confident and in control.

"Lady Anne, I hope we've not come at an inconvenient time," Charles began, "but we wanted to speak with you right away. You see, we had an encounter this morning with Lady Bloomfield."

"An *unpleasant* encounter," Alex emphasized. He unconsciously rubbed his face where she had struck him. "She seemed very upset that her niece and I were not going to be married." He was more upset by this fact than Lady Bloomfield could ever be, but he tried not to think of that.

"Lady Bloomfield, you say?" she asked. A nod from Alex confirmed it, and Lady Anne continued, "I believe Sophia's departure with her father after ending your engagement was rather widely noised about last evening. She must have heard the gossip."

"But do you know why she was so upset? Except for one brief visit after the wedding, Lady Bloomfield never even tried to contact Sophia. It seemed as though any relationship between them was over. Why would she still be angry that we are not to be married? She can't possibly care that much about her niece's reputation."

Lady Anne was seated across from them and continued to smooth out her dress rather than meet his eye. "No, you are right, Mr. Huntley," she replied. "Sophia's reputation means nothing to her, I'm very sure. I hate to be the one to tell you this. I wanted Sophia to tell you herself, but naturally now she wouldn't want to."

"Lady Anne, what are you talking about?" Alex looked at her in confusion. "What did you want . . . Sophia to tell me?" He wondered if he would ever be able to say Sophia's name without having to gather his courage first.

Lady Anne's answer remained cryptic. "I only found out myself last night. Sir Henry told me after we returned from the ball." Charles and Alex waited for Lady Anne to continue. "She mentioned yesterday morning at breakfast," she finally said, "that she needed to see her solicitor about her inheritance from her grandmother Lady Atkinson."

"Inheritance? What inheritance?" Alex asked.

Lady Anne picked at a piece of lint on the sofa in agitation. "I had wanted Sophia to be the one to tell you this, but she has inherited her grandmother's fortune. At the last computation, she has twenty-three thousand pounds, but it is very likely much more than that."

Charles and Alex looked at each other in surprise. Both quickly realized the implication: of course Lady Bloomfield would be angry if her mother had given that vast amount to Sophia instead.

"Lady Bloomfield must have hated Sophia enough to get rid of her by forcing her into a compromising situation."

"Yes, it's just as we suspected. Lady Bloomfield planned it all," Lady Anne replied as she continued to fidget nervously.

Alex didn't know how to react to this news, but the worry in Lady Anne's voice and manner was not lost on him. Between everything else racing through his mind, he was almost surprised that he noticed. If Sophia had twenty-three thousand pounds, why did Lady Anne look so tragic?

"What else?" he asked. When Lady Anne just looked at him, he asked again, "What else do you have to tell us?"

Lady Anne cleared her throat. Looking regretfully at Alex, she said, "Sir Henry accompanied Sophia to the solicitor's office and he was informed that the inheritance is only hers on the strictest of terms. It turns out that if she marries you—or anyone who's finances or reputation are questionable—then she loses everything."

Alex stood abruptly and ran his hands through his hair. He paced back and forth, forgetting the others in the room. Both Charles and Lady Anne watched him in sympathy as the hopelessness of his situation settled. After several minutes, he finally muttered to himself, "What am I going to do?" Then he turned to his friends and repeated the question. "What am I going to do?"

Lady Anne and Charles briefly shared a glance.

"I don't think there is anything you *can* do," Charles said, regret and sympathy threading through his words. There was silence in the room.

Alex narrowed his eyes in consternation as he thought on Charles's words. "Nothing I can do?" he asked his friend.

"I'm sorry, Alex." Charles turned to Lady Anne. "Thank you for taking the time to explain it all to us this morning, Lady Anne."

She walked with them to the hall to bid them farewell, expressing how truly sorry she was for the turn of events.

"Thank you for letting us know," Charles repeated. "Will we see you at Lady Moore's picnic on Saturday?"

"Of course Sir Henry and I will attend," Lady Anne responded. "Please tell Lady Everton that we'll look forward to seeing her there as well."

The two of them persisted in the mundane conversation, both pretending not to notice Alex. And throughout their exchange, Alex said nothing. His thoughts had turned inward, and Lady Anne and Charles didn't try to draw him out. Alex merely followed Charles out the door without saying good-bye.

Alex could think of nothing else but what Lady Anne had just told him. What he couldn't determine was what he could do about it. Sophia had over twenty-three thousand pounds that she would lose if she married him. Any way he looked at his situation, it was more hopeless than it had ever been. But in defiance of everything, he felt a small spark of hope.

The carriage came to a stop, and he was surprised to find himself once again with Charles on Threadneedle Street. Glancing up with a puzzled expression, Alex asked, "What are we doing here?"

Charles looked at him sympathetically, a look that said "poor Alex, can't even think straight," and gently reminded him, "You wanted to collect your family's valuables before leaving for Boxwell Court."

"No, I don't want to do that now. I'll do that later," Alex said, staring out the window. Charles gave him a long look before instructing the driver to take them home.

Twenty-Eight

William Spencer sat across from his daughter as their carriage rumbled north. They were half a day away from London now. They had made an early start, bidding the Fitzgeralds farewell before the sun had risen. But the journey north to Tissington would still take three full days. Today's journey had, for the most part, been quiet. Last night, after returning from the ball, Mr. Spencer had asked Sophia to recount everything that had happened from the moment she arrived in London until the time he had arrived himself. She had been hoarse after so much speaking. Mr. Spencer finally understood everything. After so much new information, he had hardly slept. Even now, his restless thoughts wouldn't allow him to sleep even though he was tired and the carriage rocked gently from side to side. Every so often, he would startle Sophia out of her own thoughts to ask some question or other, like details about the character and reputation of Lord and Lady Everton or what she thought of the servants in her aunt's household.

Mr. Spencer felt he understood the situation fairly thoroughly except for one unsettling point: Mr. Huntley's motives. Why did he want to marry Sophia? Was it for the money? Mr. Spencer had been sure that was the reason when he'd met Mr. Huntley at the ball, which was why Mr. Spencer had been rather brusque with the young man. But, now, after everything Sophia had told him, he wasn't so sure.

Surprising her once again, he asked, "Sophia, do you think he wants to marry you for the money you've inherited?"

"No, that I'm sure of. He only wanted to marry me for the sake of honor." She said it with conviction and without hesitation.

Her answer made him feel almost guilty for the way he had treated Mr. Huntley and he didn't want to regret the way he had handled the situation. "Why are you so sure?" he asked, doubt evident in his voice. "The money is substantial, and he tried to marry for money before."

"Remember how I told you we dined with Charles and Lucy Everton?" Mr. Spencer nodded, and she continued, "That's when I found out that he considered our engagement real. I was very displeased, but he tried to convince me to agree to the marriage. I asked him if he wanted to marry me." Sophia looked as if she didn't want to admit what Mr. Huntley's answer to that question had been. Apparently, this was one detail she had skipped over earlier. "I don't recall his exact answer, but he said a wife would be a burden and that he wouldn't have even considered marriage if it hadn't been forced upon him." After a brief hesitation, she added, "At least it proves he wasn't a fortune hunter."

Mr. Spencer nodded to acknowledge her words, but he hid his sigh of relief. He wouldn't feel bad about preventing Mr. Huntley from marrying his daughter. Obviously, Mr. Huntley felt his honor was at stake, but Mr. Spencer knew that real honor and the kind that society valued were often different things. He hoped the younger man would come to realize that too. If some misplaced sense of honor was his only motive for marrying his daughter, then taking Sophia back home to Tissington was the right thing to do. Mr. Spencer's conscience still wasn't quite comfortable, but he left it at that.

The noises of the carriage's wheels on the rutted track were all that were heard for a time. Then Sophia asked, "Father, do you think I'm being selfish?"

"Of course not, Sophia. I know you don't care about the inheritance. I'm sure you would give it up if . . ." He hesitated, not wanting to talk about whether or not his daughter was in love. So he finished lamely, ". . . er, if you felt you wanted something else more."

"Oh, um, I didn't really mean about the money. What I meant to ask was, am I being selfish by not letting Alex keep his honor by marrying me?"

It seemed a strange question to Mr. Spencer, but he had a strong conviction that society's rules of honor often bordered on the ridiculous, and he said so. He added, "Sophia, in the matter of whom you marry, you *should* be selfish—exceptionally selfish. In every other situation you can follow society's silly rules or think of everyone but yourself first, but when choosing a spouse, be selfish."

Sophia nodded but looked slightly disappointed as she turned to look out the carriage window.

Twenty-Nine

Charles and Alex returned home. As they stepped out of the carriage, Charles was surprised and a little concerned to hear Alex ask the driver to saddle his horse. Alex then hurried inside, and Charles followed close behind him.

Lucy met them as they entered the house. With just a quick hello, Alex brushed past her and went directly to his room. Trailing after him, Charles and Lucy watched Alex open his trunk, remove several things, and pack them into a satchel. His eyes were bright, but his actions were distracted. Twice he picked up his coat and then set it down again before finally picking it up and thrusting it into the satchel too.

"Where are you going, Alex?"

"Tissington."

Charles drew in a breath between his teeth. He was sure his face held an expression that showed he thought a journey to Tissington was a bad idea.

Lucy, however, was thrilled. "Oh, Alex! That's so romantic." She tugged on Charles's arm in excitement as she cried, "Sophia will never be able to resist such a gesture. I knew it would all work out."

Charles wrapped his arm around his wife to soften his contradiction. "It won't work out, and Sophia will be able to resist him. We've just found out that if Sophia marries Alex, she'll lose a fortune of at least twenty-three thousand pounds."

"No! That can't be!" Lucy exclaimed. "That has to be a mistake."

"We had an unpleasant encounter with Lady Bloomfield this morning," Charles explained, "and she first told us of it. We hurried to the Fitzgeralds' and Lady Anne confirmed it. Sophia inherited her grandmother's fortune, but the terms are very strict. If she marries Alex she'll lose it, and Lady Bloomfield will get most, if not all, of the money."

Alex was still distractedly gathering his things, but Charles watched as his wife realized the truth of the situation for the first time. Almost immediately she cried, "That's why Lady Bloomfield arranged for Alex and Sophia to be found together!"

Charles nodded in grim confirmation.

Lucy let out a deflated "ohh" and dropped her forehead onto Charles's chest. Then, remembering Alex was in the room with them, she lifted her head and asked, "If this is all true, Alex, then why are you going to Tissington?"

"To ask Sophia for her hand in marriage," he replied matter-of-factly.

"Oh, Alex." Lucy's response was all pity. "She can't marry you now."

"It will be a wasted journey, my friend," Charles added. He felt terrible that Alex was again facing gross injustice in life. But this time, the situation couldn't be rectified. "It's not your fault. You didn't know the hand you'd been dealt. But now that you *do* know, the only thing left to do is walk away."

Charles's words didn't slow Alex down, and he and Lucy watched as Alex finished loading his satchel and turned to face his two friends. He looked to be at a loss for words but finally made an effort to explain. "I have to try. I thought that she said no because . . . because—" He stammered as he tried to convey his thoughts. "Because she didn't want me. But if that isn't true, if there is *any* other reason, then maybe I still have a chance."

Charles knew he didn't have a chance. "It's a lost cause. You can't ask her to give up everything. You will travel all the way there to be told no again. Don't do it, Alex. Don't go." Lucy stood at Charles's side, nodding in agreement.

Doubt clouded Alex's expression for a brief moment. But he pushed aside Charles's advice. "I've already lost her. I have nothing more to lose."

Looking up with determination in his eyes once more, he repeated, "I have to try." Charles was about to contradict him again, but Alex cut him off. "Why are you trying to talk me out of this? Last night you wanted me to go to Sophia and try again."

"The money changes everything. You know that. I just don't want to see you disappointed again."

"I can't be any more disappointed than I am now," Alex responded, letting out a deep sigh. "I know that she won't have me, Charles, but I have to try anyway."

Charles hated the impossibility of the situation but he knew he had done his best to talk Alex out of more heartache, so he didn't argue the point any further. Instead, he stepped aside and pulled Lucy with him. With his free arm, he gestured to the door and said, "Give our regards to Miss Spencer." He didn't agree with Alex's decision, but he conceded the point anyway.

With a slight half grin in response, Alex walked past Charles and Lucy. He turned back and said, "Thank you." Alex looked like he wanted to say more, but he let out a deep sigh instead.

Finally, he clapped Charles on the shoulder. "And by the way, you were right."

Charles wished more than anything that he hadn't been right. Without much hope, he said, "I hope, in this case, that I am wrong."

Charles and Lucy accompanied Alex outside and bade him a safe journey. They watched as he mounted his horse and rode off. He passed through their large iron gate, turned his horse north, and was soon out of sight.

Lucy interlaced her fingers through Charles's and turned to look at him. "It might work, you know."

Charles shook his head. "No, it won't. He'll be back here in a week, more depressed than he's ever been. I don't know how he'll pick up the pieces and carry on this time."

"You're probably right," Lucy said, "but perhaps we are underestimating Sophia. She might love Alex enough to give up that inheritance." She looked at Charles lovingly. "I know that I would have made that choice for you if I'd had to."

Charles smiled back at his wife. "And I would have done for you exactly what Alex is doing for Miss Spencer." With a rueful look, he couldn't help but add, "That might even be worse. If she gives up a fortune, surely they will end up resenting each other. I fear it wouldn't be a happy marriage."

Lucy looked deflated again. There didn't seem to be any way for Alex and Sophia to end up happy and together.

Thirty

It had been quite late when they had finally arrived home, and Sophia found it difficult to sleep. Despite tossing and turning well into the night, she was still up before the sun. By the time she was dressed in her riding habit and heading toward the stable, the world was just visible through the gray light of dawn. It was quiet in the stable. Pearl was in her stall and Sophia walked over to her.

"Hello, Pearl," she said in a hushed voice. Pearl perked up and sniffed and snorted in response. Sophia leaned her forehead against Pearl's. Three days of being confined in the carriage as well as missing sleep had Sophia's emotions much too near the surface. "I won't leave you again," she whispered to Pearl. "I missed you too much." She broken down in quiet sobs with her arms around the horse's neck.

She knew Thomas was often up early and could come into the stable at any time, so she quieted herself as quickly as she could, taking deep, shaky breaths. She brushed her hands down Pearl's mane and said quietly, "We'll go for a lovely long ride this morning. And every day. It will be like I've never left." She took her time brushing Pearl down and saddling her, giving the sun a chance to come up a little higher.

She knew she had missed her home and her horse more than she had taken the time to think about. Missing her father had been an obvious thing; he had been on her mind a lot while she was away. When she hadn't received any letters from him, she had missed him more than ever. But she hadn't spared much thought for Pearl during her stay in London. Now that she was back, she knew how much she had missed her horse. She had also missed her home, where she was always comfortable and in control.

There were no hidden rules here. Everything was straightforward. She didn't have to impress anyone here; she was accepted just as she was, and no one was plotting against her. She was perfectly safe.

Even as these thoughts comforted her, she admitted to herself that something felt different. Home didn't feel quite the same. Somehow, it felt less like home than it had before. But no, she reassured herself, nothing had changed.

"I've changed," she said out loud, and her own voice startled her.

Perhaps I have changed, she thought, *but now that I'm home I'll change back*. She had only been gone a month. Surely any change in that short amount of time wouldn't be permanent. This was where she would be for the rest of her life. She was sure that she would quickly find herself feeling the same as she always had in no time. Feeling more depressed than reassured, she set off on the ride she had been anticipating.

Sophia was right where she wanted to be. It was a beautiful morning, and she was riding Pearl. She was on her favorite ride too. She started by heading west. Then after going through Dovedale Wood, she wound her way south and east. Once she reached the far southern edge of Sir Henry's property, she turned back toward home, going from one beautiful hilltop to the next.

Reaching the top of each hill was the best part of her ride. She loved clear days like today when she could see for miles into the distance. She loved the view when she was finally above every obstacle and her eyes could glimpse every part of the path she had taken. She would always stop on the hilltops and take everything in—the road, the river, the clusters of houses, the pastures, and the fields. She had done this very ride a hundred times, and the beauty of the views from each vantage point never failed to draw her in. Until today.

Today she couldn't feel enthusiastic about the beauty, the hilltops, or even the thrill of riding Pearl at a full gallop. She had pulled Pearl to a stop when they came over the first rise. Facing Tissington and looking at the beautiful place she called home, all she felt was miserable.

But this was what she had looked forward to! On her three-day carriage ride home from London, she hadn't had much to be excited about when they arrived. This had been the one thing that she thought would distract her from her melancholy mood.

Perhaps she was too tired to enjoy herself.

Halfway through her morning ride and looking over a scene that never failed to cheer her, Sophia felt close to tears again.

She tried not to think of Alex, but she couldn't help wondering if he was home by then. She remembered the day in the garden at Dalton House when he had told her about Boxwell Court. She had formed a picture in her mind as he'd described it, and she thought of that now. What if she were on a ride with Alex at her side, overlooking the scene she pictured in her mind? She pushed that thought away without answering. It was useless to wonder about such things. Actually, she was glad that she didn't really know what Boxwell Court looked like. She didn't want to know what she was missing.

Sophia remembered her first impression of Alex and how wrong she had been. She almost smiled at how she had thought him such a villain in the beginning. But actually Alex was wonderful. Yes, he had been quite angry when they spoke before the wedding, but now she realized that he must have been under an immense amount of strain to lose his temper as he had. She wished she had stayed. For the first time since she ran away from the wedding, she regretted it. She had been so proud of herself for finally making a choice of her own, but if she had married Alex that day, they would be together now. He surely would have been angry when he discovered the inheritance was lost, but the marriage would have bound them together, and Alex was reasonable enough that he wouldn't have blamed her eventually.

It was too late now. If she had agreed to marry him knowing that she would lose her inheritance, she would have been to blame, and he would never forgive her.

Tears started falling again, and Sophia resolved once more to stop thinking about Alex. She urged Pearl down the hill and decided to think about how she would use grandmother's money. She did love riding, and her reunion with Pearl had her thinking that perhaps she would like to build up a stable full of fine horses. She would have to really work to build up her enthusiasm for the project, but at least it kept her mind busy for a time before it inevitably drifted back to Alex. She couldn't help thinking about how much she missed him and what she could have said or done differently that would have resulted in a happy ending.

Distracted, Sophia held the reins loosely. She didn't notice Pearl's increasing speed as she continued down the hill. When Pearl shifted suddenly to avoid something in her path, Sophia shot out of the saddle and flew through the air, landing hard and rolling several times. The breath was knocked from her, and she lay motionless and dazed for several seconds, trying to recover.

Pain in her foot let Sophia know she had injured it. She sat up slowly and removed her boot to examine her aching foot. It looked fine, but it hurt terribly. Looking around, she saw Pearl had stopped several feet away. Sophia stood up on her uninjured foot and hopped over to her, still holding her boot. She gently placed her injured foot in the stirrup and tried to lift herself up into the saddle, but the pain startled her, and she fell back down.

Sophia desperately wished she had paid better attention while she was riding. She had never been thrown before, and it was completely her fault. Actually, it was Mr. Alexander Huntley's fault too. If she weren't so pathetically in love with him, she would have stayed on her horse.

She knew she needed to get home so her father could look at her injury, and the only way for her to get home was by riding. She put her injured foot on the ground and tried to balance on it while she put her other foot in the stirrup, but it was impossible.

Sophia looked around again and saw that they were at the bottom of the hill near Sir Henry's south pasture, which had a tree stump about a hundred yards away. If she went to that side of the pasture she would be quite near the road, and she didn't want anyone to see her, especially if that someone were Martha. But she felt that the stump was her best chance for being able to mount Pearl, so she hopped to it as quickly as she could on her uninjured foot.

It was much farther and harder than she thought it would be. She stopped several times to lean on Pearl and catch her breath. With her leg aching from unaccustomed use, Sophia finally reached the tree stump and levered herself up. She tried again to climb into the saddle, but her injured foot hurt worse than before. It had swollen up quite a bit during her hop, and she still couldn't put pressure on it. Sophia sat down on the ground, feeling discouraged. She knew that if she could get on Pearl's back, she would be home in no time. Perhaps if she rested for a bit she could make one last effort to get in the saddle and be on her way.

Thirty-One

It was just past midday, and Alex was sure he must be close. He pulled out his notes as he came to the end of the hedge that bordered the field on his left. Before leaving the Inn in Brailsford that morning, he had written down detailed directions from the proprietor. He had felt a sense of constant urgency for the last three days, and he really didn't want to get lost now.

Reading over what he had written that morning, he saw that the road would curve to the right, and then he would take the first left. After a mile or so, the road would fork around a walled pasture. He would stay to the left and then, over the next rise, he would see Tissington. Slipping the directions back in his pocket, Alex went over his plan again.

The innkeeper in Brailsford had said the only lodging in Tissington was a couple of rooms above the town shop. Alex's plan was to find his way to the village shop and ask for a room first thing. It would probably seem odd for a traveler to be hiring a room this early in the day, but he would avoid questions if he could. He needed to quickly clean away any dirt he had acquired while traveling. Then he would ask where the Spencers lived.

That was the easy part. The difficult part of his plan was what he would say to Sophia when he saw her. His ride the past three days had been spent trying to solve this very problem, but he couldn't seem to find an eloquent way to ask, "Will you please give up your fortune and marry me?"

One thing he would tell Sophia was that he loved her. He didn't have any great hope that it would be enough. The last time he saw Sophia, she had quite coolly rejected him. But he hadn't told her he loved her, a mistake he wouldn't make this time.

As he continued on his journey, Alex tried to determine when his feelings for Sophia had turned to love. Charles had thought it was much sooner than Alex had admitted it to himself. He wanted to pinpoint a moment in time so he could tell Sophia, "I've loved you since . . ." But he couldn't finish the sentence to his satisfaction. At the earliest, he had first felt a protective sort of regard for her after she had disappeared from the wedding. And at the latest there was devastating heartbreak after she left London with her father. Truthfully, it was sometime between those two events that Alex had fallen in love without even knowing it.

Alex was busy casting his mind back over the past few weeks when he noticed a saddled horse without a rider in the pasture up ahead. He looked around, but he didn't see anyone. As he rode closer, though, he thought he saw someone on the ground on the other side of the horse.

He urged his horse faster and jumped the low hedge into the pasture, quickly coming around the white horse. Sophia was sitting on the ground, leaning against a tree stump. Alex dismounted quickly. Obviously, she had heard the approach of a rider and looked up, wary of whom it might be. Her jaw dropped when she recognized him, and she tried to quickly scramble to her feet. She wasn't successful. She grimaced and sat down hard again. Her face was pale, and Alex noticed beads of perspiration on her forehead.

"Sophia! What has happened?" Before she could answer, he guessed, "Were you thrown from your horse?"

Sophia didn't answer right away, a pained look still on her face, but she finally gave a nod. "It was more like I fell than was thrown," she admitted.

"Where are you hurt?"

"Just my foot," she said, pointing down to her right foot. "If I could get back on my horse, I could ride home, but I can't put any weight on my foot. I was just resting for a bit before trying again."

"Let me help you." Alex put one knee on the ground as he scooped Sophia up in his arms. She instinctively put her arms around his neck as he rose to his feet. He suddenly realized the intimacy of the moment, and he froze.

Sophia was in his arms with her arms wrapped around him. This was everything he wanted! But they hadn't resolved anything yet. They had hardly even spoken.

It felt so right to have her in his arms, yet Alex was distraught. This might be the only chance he would ever have to hold her.

Truly, he had wanted to hold her like this since the day of the wedding. When the streets of London had swallowed her up, he had experienced that first unfamiliar need to protect her. She was finally in his arms, and he wanted to keep it that way—forever.

Sophia was staring into his eyes while these thoughts occurred to him. She seemed to overcome her surprise at being picked up and said, "If you'll just . . ." She leaned toward her horse and reached an arm out to steady herself with the saddle. "Yes, just set me here." Alex's arms fell away as she slid into the saddle and adjusted her seat.

Alex saw her grimace in pain again. "Does it hurt very badly?" he asked.

"I just jostled it," she said with her eyes still closed.

"Would you rather I carry you?" Sophia shook her head, but Alex was insistent. "I could easily carry you, and we could lead the horses."

Sophia opened her eyes and looked down at Alex. "Alex, what are you doing here?"

He paused as he thought about his purpose and how Sophia would react. "I forgot to tell you something."

Sophia just looked at him expectantly, but Alex couldn't say it yet. "I realized that I had to tell you. But you were gone, so I came here to tell you."

Alex didn't continue, and the silence lengthened.

"What do you have to tell me?" Sophia finally asked.

Alex's gaze had drifted away to the horizon, and it jerked back up to Sophia. He held her gaze for a moment longer before saying what was in his heart. "I love you. I forgot to tell you that I love you."

"Oh," Sophia said. And she looked away.

Alex's heart sank. He hadn't expected any similar declaration from her, but he had hoped for it just the same. He had come an awfully long way, though, so he didn't give up just yet. Reaching out, he clasped her hand. Sophia turned back and looked at him. Her eyes were filled with tears that were about to brim over.

"Sophia, don't cry." He didn't know why she was crying, but all he wanted to do was pull her back into his arms and protect her.

"I forgot to tell you something too, Alex," she admitted. "If we marry, I'll lose my grandmother's inheritance." She paused and then tacked on, "And it's substantial."

"I know."

"You know?"

"Yes, Lady Anne told me. Well, first Lady Bloomfield accosted me with the information, but Lady Anne later clarified it. You see, I saw your aunt in the street the morning you left, and she slapped me for not marrying you." Sophia's eyes went wide. "It was no less than I deserved really. I needed some sense slapped into me for letting you go.

"That was when I first learned that you even had a fortune to lose. Lady Anne later explained that your grandmother wanted her money carefully looked after and that you would lose it if you married a fortune hunter like me." Clasping her hand between both of his own, Alex said. "I want to marry you anyway."

Sophia's tears fell then. "I knew you would still try to convince me, Alex, but it's no use. You've thought from the start that you have to marry me to save my reputation."

Alex couldn't resist then. He pulled Sophia out of the saddle and into his arms. He gently lowered her to the ground, being careful to help support her so she wouldn't bump her injured foot. Keeping his arms around her, he said, "I don't care if it's the right or wrong thing to do. I want to marry you because I love you more than any reputation."

As Sophia balanced on one foot, she explained, "But I can't marry you without any dowry at all. I would be a burden to you, and you would never be able to restore Boxwell Court."

Alex put a finger under her chin and tilted her face up. When her eyes met his, he said, "I love you more than Boxwell Court."

"But the money—" she said desperately.

"I love you far more than twenty-three thousand pounds," Alex interrupted. He brushed a stray lock of hair behind her ear, feeling more protective of her than ever. "I would give up everything for you. Everything," he repeated, "even my pride, by asking you to give it all up too . . . for me." Alex let his words hang there while he waited for her response.

"I love you too." Her voice broke as she said it, but Alex had never heard anything more beautiful. He tightened his hold around her and lifted her off the ground. Her arms came up around his neck again as Alex held her tightly in his arms. It felt like heaven to him, and he closed his eyes as he savored the feeling. It was immense relief to have her in his arms—absolutely exquisite that she was returning the embrace.

He never wanted to let her go, but Sophia pulled her head back to look at him. "I shouldn't agree to this. I'm going to make your life so much harder with nothing to contribute." As she said it, she made a slight effort to pull away, but Alex didn't loosen his grip one bit. If anything, he locked her tighter in his arms and quickly pressed his mouth to hers. For Alex, the kiss was the only thing left he could think of to convince her, but once their lips, met he was the one convinced. This was his fate.

The kiss softened, and he felt Sophia's response as she sighed and her arms came back around his neck. He made no attempt to end the kiss, and it was several blissful moments before Sophia pulled back again. Her beautiful blush and guilty smile made him love her even more. He couldn't live without this woman.

"Sophia, I want nothing more in this world than to marry you. Will you agree to a real engagement this time?"

She nodded her head in response and whispered affectionately, "Yes." Her eyes were still teary, and she shook her head gently as if she couldn't believe it herself. "This is the most selfish thing I could ever do, because you deserve so much more . . ." She looked almost exultant as her face broke into a wide smile. "But I'm going to do it anyway."

Alex didn't quite know how to express himself with words. But his smile matched hers as he spun in a circle with Sophia in his arms.

Sophia looked down a bit self-consciously and then glanced back at Alex through her lashes. "You can set me down now."

"I'd better not. I don't want you to hurt your foot again." Alex shifted her to the side and reached down to scoop her higher into his arms once more. He was about to lift her onto her saddle, but in this position he couldn't resist kissing her again. Sophia wound her arms tighter around his neck. It was several minutes before he finally set her on her horse.

Thirty-Two

$\mathcal{A}$s they set off across the pasture, Sophia was unaware of anything else but Alex. Even the constant throbbing in her foot couldn't keep the smile off her face. She didn't want to break the connection between them and wished they could at least hold hands, but she knew it was better not to. She gripped the reins with two hands, not wanting to fall off Pearl again. It had been humiliating, but being rescued by Alex had surpassed every romantic idea she'd ever had.

She had made the most selfish decision of her life by agreeing to marry Alex. But she wouldn't let herself regret it. Her father had told her that this decision was the one time she could justify being selfish. The only thing to keep her from being perfectly happy was the thought that Alex might one day regret it.

Sophia led the way back to Tissington, and as they rode, Alex reassured her again that they didn't need her inheritance. "Perhaps I've led you to believe that Boxwell Court is worse off than it really is. Honestly, we'll be fine. We'll just have to wait a few years before we redecorate the drawing room."

"Are you sure, Alex? I'd hate for you to be sorry for this later."

"I don't need anything but you," he said, and Sophia lost her breath with the romance of it all.

He continued to reassure her of his love, and Sophia's doubts were gone before the ride was over.

Sophia and Alex returned to her home. He helped her inside, and they sat down together in the drawing room with hands clasped, which was where her father found them when he arrived a short time later from his morning visits.

Sophia's first impulse when her father entered the room was to pull her hand out of Alex's grasp. She resisted the impulse, however, since her father might as well know how things stood.

In a too cheerful voice, she said, "Hello, Father. Alex has arrived." It was unnecessary, of course, but she couldn't think of anything more pertinent to say.

Sophia noticed that her father looked almost relieved, which surprised her.

"Hello, Mr. Huntley," he said, coming farther into the room. "You've come all the way from London to visit us, have you?"

Sophia heard the amusement in her father's voice, and Alex must have noticed it as well. He seemed confused at being received positively. "Yes, I had to come see your daughter . . . but perhaps you'd better see to her injury first."

All thoughts and discussion were set aside as Alex directed Mr. Spencer to the more urgent matter of Sophia's swollen foot. After a quick examination, he pronounced it sprained and carefully wrapped it, embarrassing Sophia by making her recount what had happened. She was mortified to relate how she had fallen off Pearl in front of Alex.

"You fell off?" her father asked, puzzled.

Her face turned red at having to repeat it. "Yes. I was distracted while I was riding, and I fell off."

"You've never fallen off before. What had you so preoccupied?"

Sophia involuntarily glanced at Alex and back at her father. From Alex's expression, she knew he knew, so she merely mumbled, "I wasn't concentrating, I suppose."

Her father looked back and forth between the two of them. "Is everything settled between the two of you?"

Alex answered, "Yes, sir," while Sophia nodded.

Sophia and Alex both waited nervously for her father's response. He finally gave them a smile. "What a relief."

Alex and Sophia were both surprised at his reaction, so he explained, "When we first began our journey from London, I thought Sophia was feeling down because of the ordeal she had been through. But I have never seen my daughter as quiet and sad as she has been for the last three days. When I saw her leave for her ride this morning without any enthusiasm at all, the thought crossed my mind that we had made a mistake by leaving London. Thank you, Mr. Huntley, for coming all this way to set things right."

Alex responded to her father, but he looked tenderly at Sophia as he did so. "It was my mistake, sir. I should never have let her leave so easily."

Sophia thought her father might have contradicted Alex just to be polite, but he didn't. "I hope you'll stay for dinner, Mr. Huntley," he merely said.

"Yes. Thank you." He looked curious as he asked, "I thought you would be much more discouraging of us. If you don't mind me asking, why are you letting Sophia abandon her inheritance to marry me instead?"

"Her mother and I made a similar decision when we married," he replied. He paused as if fondly remembering that time, and then, smiling warmly at the pair of them, he said, "Perhaps Sophia can tell you about it," and stepped from the room.

Her father couldn't have said anything to make Sophia happier. With her foot propped up on a chair and Alex holding her hand, she told him all about how her parents had fallen in love and what they had given up for each other.

She had always wanted to find love like her parents had. She knew she loved Alex and was pleased that her father could see that they were as in love as he and her mother had been when they had sacrificed so much to be together. She finally had a true love story. It was even better than she had imagined it would be.

Alex told her about his family. Although he hadn't had many opportunities to be close to them in the last few years, he hoped that would change once they were married. He wanted Sophia to know his mother and sisters and love them too.

That led to talk of their future, and they realized they had many decisions to make. Luckily, they were both in agreement that although Alex still had the special license he had procured for their wedding in London, they would have the bans read for three weeks at the Tissington Parish before being married by Reverend Henley.

❧

Lady Anne was pleased to be returning to Tissington Park. Several months in the country would be a nice respite after London, especially the episode at the end with Sophia and Mr. Huntley. She had been furious at Mr. Spencer for taking his daughter back to Tissington until Sir Henry had finally explained the conditions of Sophia's inheritance, which he had learned from the solicitor. Lady Anne had been shocked at Lady Atkinson's eccentricity and then appalled at her own machinations, which had made the situation worse. She hadn't done anything wrong knowingly, but that thought wouldn't make her feel less guilty when she saw Sophia and her father at church.

Lady Anne had almost decided to skip services her first week back. But she had a responsibility in the village, and part of that was setting a good example for the others in the parish. So she sat with Sir Henry in their pew at the front. She even determined to stop Sophia afterward and apologize for what had happened. Not that it was her fault, but she *had* convinced Sophia to agree to a false engagement that she had known would lead to feelings for Mr. Huntley. Even though Sophia had resisted, Lady Anne was sure that she had fallen in love with Mr. Huntley and now was suffering from a broken heart.

When the vicar announced the intention of Miss Sophia Spencer and Mr. Alexander Huntley to wed, Lady Anne's jaw dropped in surprise. She turned back to stare in shock at a smiling Sophia sitting next to Mr. Huntley. She didn't hear a word of the sermon as she tried to work out how they had solved an unsolvable problem.

After services, Lady Anne wasted no time in approaching them immediately. "Mr. Huntley, how are you here with Sophia?" she demanded. "I thought your situation was impossible."

He gave Sophia an affectionate look before answering, "We decided to make it possible. Sophia has agreed to give up her inheritance and marry me anyway."

Lady Anne didn't know how to react. On the one hand, giving up that amount of money was a ridiculous thing for anyone to do, but on the other hand, she had been pushing these two together. She couldn't decide if she should scold them or celebrate her triumph.

Sir Henry decided the matter for her. "Congratulations, my dear. Your matchmaking skills are beyond compare." He turned to the young couple and said, "We'll have to enjoy your company before you marry and leave us. Are you free today? We would love to have you join us for dinner."

Sophia nodded, but Lady Anne caught her hesitantly looking

in her direction. Lady Anne realized she must have looked disapproving and quickly changed her expression to show her support. She took the invitation for dinner into her capable hands, including Mr. Spencer as well. And as they walked down the path away from the church, she said, "I knew it from the beginning. I knew that the two of you would make a perfect match. Sir Henry can tell you, can't you, dear? How I said it was only a matter of time before you both realized you were in love."

Thirty-Three

Alex and Sophia's second wedding day was cloudy but mild. Tissington was a small parish, and nearly everyone in it would be attending the wedding. Alex had been staying with the Fitzgeralds for the last three weeks and had seemed to enjoy his time in Tissington immensely, but he had admitted to Sophia that he wouldn't be sorry to return to Boxwell Court after such a long absence. He had shown her the letter that his mother had written to him in response to his announcement of marriage. His mother and his sister's family were planning to visit Boxwell Court next month in order to meet his new bride. The thought of it made Sophia a bit nervous, but mostly she was excited to get to know Alex's family.

With all they had to look forward to, there were still several responsibilities that couldn't be neglected. Sophia had taken time to write a lengthy letter to Mr. Wilson while her sprained foot was healing. She had told him of her decision to marry Alexander

Huntley despite the fact that Mr. Wilson and her grandmother would surely not approve, stating that she was giving up all rights to the inheritance. She also explained to him the problems she had faced with her aunt, hoping that in some way it would help him to be forewarned while dealing with her.

Because of her injured foot, Sophia had been unable to help her father purchase a horse to replace Pearl, who would be leaving with her after the wedding. Alex had accompanied Mr. Spencer to Sheffield, and after a long day they had come home with a beautiful horse. The only fault Sophia could find with him was that he was too docile, but her father was pleased.

Feeling that all the loose ends had been neatly tied off, she was ready to marry the man she loved and begin their life together.

With a barely noticeable limp, Sophia and her father walked to the church, where Alex was waiting for them.

Everyone in Tissington walked to church. It would be absurd to drive such a short distance. A carriage at their little parish was an unusual sight. But there, just pulling up to the entrance, was a black carriage.

"Father, whose carriage do you suppose that is?" Sophia asked.

"Er . . . I'm not sure." Her father seemed to think for a moment of any wedding guests that would possibly arrive in a carriage and finally asked, "Do you think Alex's family has come for the wedding?"

As they got closer, and Sophia realized that she had seen that carriage before. "That's Mr. Wilson's carriage!"

Mr. Wilson himself emerged from it. With a look of relief on his face as he saw them approach, he said, "Hello, Miss Spencer. I see I've arrived just in time. I knew we were cutting it quite close, so I instructed the driver to come directly to the church." He seemed tired but pleased as he waited for a reply.

Confused, Sophia looked around for a moment as if somehow the scenery would give her a clue as to why Mr. Wilson was here.

"Have you come all this way for the wedding, Mr. Wilson?" her father asked, looking as confused as Sophia felt. "That's very kind of you."

"I would be pleased to attend the ceremony, but my real purpose here is to sanction Miss Spencer's choice for her husband, which, according to the terms of Lady Atkinson's will, must be accomplished before the wedding takes place. I'm just relieved I arrived in time. I had to oversee the removal of Lady Bloomfield from Miss Spencer's house in town before I could leave. I didn't quite realize how little time that would leave me."

Sophia felt a brief wave of panic. Had she not been clear when she wrote to Mr. Wilson? He must have misunderstood somehow. "Oh no!" she cried. "I'm afraid you've come all this way for nothing. I'm so sorry it wasn't readily understood from my letter, but I decided to marry Mr. Huntley, so I know I have to give up grandmother's inheritance."

Alex came out of the church then, along with several others who had been waiting inside for the ceremony to begin. He must have heard Sophia's dismayed voice because he hurried to her side. "What's happened? You're not hurt again, are you?"

"No, no, I'm not hurt," she quick reassured ask. "It's just that Mr. Wilson has come all the way from London for nothing. I must not have explained our situation clearly in my letter, and I feel dreadful that I've caused him so much trouble."

When Sophia said Mr. Wilson's name, Alex glanced up in surprise. In complete astonishment, he cried, "Mr. Wilson, what are you doing here?"

Mr. Wilson grinned, which was another surprise for both Sophia and Alex. "I see you haven't discovered that you two have a mutual acquaintance—me." Turning to Sophia, he said, "I have been Mr. Huntley's solicitor for almost five years now. I have been employed by him to help deal with the numerous legal matters that naturally occur when running a large estate. I have even been to Boxwell Court on several occasions."

Sophia and Alex looked at each other as the truth dawned on them. "We have the same solicitor," Alex said unnecessarily.

Now that everyone understood their connection, Mr. Wilson continued to address Sophia, "Knowing Mr. Huntley as well as I do, I don't think you could make a better choice. His character has always impressed me, and he is financially astute." Sophia thought she could detect something in Mr. Wilson's voice that indicated he thought she was quite lucky to have snared Mr. Huntley. But if that was the case, he hid it well. "As your marriage is taking place today," he said matter-of-factly, "you will have full access to your inheritance, including all the investments, immediately."

Mr. Wilson's somber manner couldn't diminish Sophia's excitement. She clasped Alex's arm with both hands and exclaimed, "Alex, we get to keep it—my grandmother's money is ours!" Alex looked more stunned than overjoyed, but the other wedding guests who had heard all began talking and congratulating the pair.

Reverend Henley finally brought order to the group. His voice was quiet, but he raised an authoritative hand that somehow caught most everyone's attention. "It's time to begin the ceremony," he announced. "Please show reverence as you enter the house of the Lord."

It was still hard to remain subdued, but most of them followed Reverend Henley up the path. Alex clasped Sophia's hand and gently pulled her back so that they would trail behind the others. He stopped Sophia before they followed everyone else inside.

"You know," Alex said, "I'm almost disappointed. I had begun to feel pleased that you didn't have a fortune."

With disbelief evident in her voice, Sophia asked, "You're not really, are you? Think of how much easier it will be."

Alex shrugged and looked down at the ground. "Well, yes," he admitted reluctantly, "I don't deny that it will be much easier to have a fortune than not. But now I'm a fortune hunter again. If your inheritance had been taken away, I would have been the opposite of a fortune hunter."

Sophia looked at Alex speculatively from the corners of her eyes. Then looking away again and keeping her tone regretful, she responded, "I suppose you're right. That's how everyone will see it now. You are a fortune hunter, and I got caught in your snare—that's what they'll all say." Dismay colored her voice and Sophia finished with a sigh. She glanced at Alex, who had moved a step away. His hands were in his pockets, his eyes staring at the ground. He seemed discouraged at the thought of being labeled a fortune hunter once more.

"In fact," Sophia continued, "you might even say that your reputation is ruined." Alex looked up at her sharply at the familiar phrase. When his gaze met Sophia's, she was smiling mischievously. "Luckily for you, I love you more than your reputation." And with that Alex stepped forward and pulled her into his arms and kissed her. Sophia didn't care what anyone else thought about it. Not one bit.

Sophia finally pulled back and looked into Alex's eyes. She thought about their last wedding and the events immediately preceding it. They hadn't known each other at all, and the only thing between them had been a misunderstanding. In the churchyard in London, Alex had yelled at her, and she had run away.

Now they were standing in the churchyard in Tissington. Alex was gazing at her with so much love that it reached to her soul. Running away was the last thing on her mind. Instead, she stood on her toes to kiss him one more time before taking his hand and pulling him into the church to begin their life together.

Discussion Questions

1. Sophia worries that she is selfish, but what are her true character flaws?

2. Alex tells her they have no choice but to marry, then states that they either get married or her reputation is ruined. Why does he view that as "not a choice"?

3. Lady Anne and Alex conspire to make the fake engagement real without telling Sophia. Is their plotting justified because their motives are for Sophia's good?

4. Charles and Lucy also plan their ball without telling Alex about it. Is their plotting justified because they are acting out of friendship?

5. Sophia's father tells her to be selfish when choosing a spouse. How have his experiences contributed to his philosophy?

6. Would Alex and Sophia have had their happily ever after without Sophia's inheritance?

7. Sophia is proud of herself for her independence when she runs away from the wedding, but later comes to regret that decision when she realizes she can't marry Alex. Would they have found the same happiness if she had gone through with the marriage the first time?

About the Author

Paula Kremser focused on a career in science for several years after graduating from Brigham Young University. When she moved to England, Paula seized the opportunity to focus on her love of the Regency era. The enchantment of the aristocracy and the fascinating stories from every stately home she visits have been both research and inspiration for her first novel. Paula stays quite busy raising her young family of four children in Stokenchurch, England.